THE PEABODY LIBRARY

Columbia City, Indiana

James, Margaret
Lucy's cottage

FEB 19 '82	DATE DUE		
FEB 19 '82	JUN 21 '82	MY 2'90	
FEB 26 '82	JUL 12 '82		
MAR 8 '82	JUL 22 '82	JE 29 '90 JY 13 '90	
MAR 10 '82	JUL 29 '82	DE 6'93	
MAR 29 '82	AUG 13 '82	AP -5 '94	
APR 14 '82	SEP 7 '82	AP 1 '95	
APR 14 '82	OCT 8 '82		
MAY 3 '82	NOV 8 '82		
MAY 12 '82	MAR 14 '84		
MAY 26 '82	MAY 11 '84		
JUN 4 '82	AUG 3 '84		
GAYLORD 234	MAY 24 '84	PRINTED IN U. S. A.	

Lucy's Cottage

Lucy's Cottage

Margaret James

ST. MARTIN'S PRESS
NEW YORK

Library of Congress Cataloging in Publication Data

James, Margaret.
    Lucy's cottage.

    I.   Title.
PR6052.E533L8   823'.914   80-28948
ISBN 0-312-50006-8

ACKNOWLEDGMENTS

I am indebted to the following authors, whose scholarship not only helped me to obtain facts about Victorian England, but also painted a vivid picture of that period, which enabled me to write this book: –

Life Below Stairs.	Frank E. Hugget.
The Victorian Home.	Jenni Calder.
The Victorian Gentleman.	Michael Brander.
Leisure & Pleasure in the 19th Century.	Stella Margetson.
Time to Spare in Victorian England.	John Lowerson and John Myerscough.
Handbook of English Costume in the 19th Century.	C. Willett Cunnington and Phillis Cunnington.
Crinolines and Crimping Irons.	Christina Walkley and Vanda Foster.
Book of Household Management.	Isabella Beeton.
Costume and Fashion 1760–1920.	Jack Cassin-Scott.
English Costume of the 19th Century.	James Laver.

P.B.

PROLOGUE

The girl's breath was tearing at her throat, like a self-inflicted wound, her lungs fighting a battle too great for them.

It felt to her as though she had been running for hours, but what was left of reason told her that it couldn't have been more than ten minutes or so since she had seen the strange shapes coming towards her, and had fled from Dory's Meadow and across the village green.

She had hoped the church might offer sanctuary from her pursuers, whoever they were, but St Paul's lay stolid and locked, its windows like blind eyes, uncaring and indifferent to her terror.

It was so dark. She couldn't see a hand in front of her, but her tormentors had lanterns to guide them. She had seen them; small, bobbing splashes to illuminate their paths and catch their victim in the beams.

By now, she had crossed the stream, feeling shallow water suck at her ankles as if it wanted to hold her still. She stumbled on wet stones, dragging herself by sheer desperation to the point where the secretive tangle of Farthing Wood began.

From the beginning, she had never liked the wood. It had seemed hostile to her, even in bright daylight. On an autumn night, with just a hint of moonlight, it filled her with primitive dread, but the fast-moving steps behind her left her no choice.

She managed the last few yards without falling, entering the wood in panic. Her arms were stretched out in front of her, but, despite this, she soon collided with a tree, holding on to the trunk for precious seconds, gulping in air. Then on again. On and on, fumbling between oak, ash, elm and aspen. The trees were unfriendly, barring her way. The spiky bushes and shrubs laid traps for her. They didn't want her to escape.

When she reached the first clearing, she knew that she was finished. The thudding of shoes had stopped and she turned, seeing the semi-circle of lights bathing her fear for all to see. She could hear an owl somewhere. Everyone said that it was an unlucky bird; a creature of ill omen. There were other things too; a rustle here and there; the snapping of a twig. Above her, a slight wind moved the dying leaves, making them sigh.

" Wh . . . what do you want?"

She got the words out at last, knowing that they were no more than a gasp: knowing too that she would get no answer.

Even now, she couldn't tell how many people there were, nor whether they were men or women. The outlines appeared to waver, merging together in the oddest way. They seemed to have no faces either, just eyes staring at her through slits, watching her crumbling to pieces before them.

" Wh . . . what is it? Why are you following me?"

Her voice trailed off as one of the group detached itself and hurried towards her. She had no strength left to run, hypnotised as the figure reached her. Her mouth was open, ugly with the horror of it all, when she could see in the glare of the raised lanthorn nothing more than a pair of eyes. Greedy eyes, fixed on hers, demanding from her more than mere fear.

She was grey now, trembling and weak, knowing that her knees were giving way and that soon she would lie on the damp carpet of earth and moss, totally at the mercy of the people who had trapped her.

Then she felt the pain. It was like nothing she had ever known before. A hurt so unbearable that it enveloped her completely, making her forget the night, the noises and those all about her. She wanted to scream, but she couldn't. The pain had made her numb, stifling the last ounce of breath in her.

Hands reached for her and there were murmurings, but her senses were failing. She was aware that she was being raised up, but she no longer wanted to protest or demand who was doing these things to her. It was too late.

After a while, the blessed state of unconsciousness passed away, and the torment was back, grinding into her like splintered glass, agony filling every fibre of her being.

The voices had started again, low and indistinguishable. She was lifted once more, this time into some enclosed space. The cool night air was gone; so were the sounds of the wood.

When she was put down, she no longer had the will to beg for pity. The fingers which lay across her stomach were covered in a warm, sticky substance, but it didn't seem to matter. Everything was fading, like a dream upon waking. She was floating, almost carefree, and no longer afraid.

She lay very still, the fight over. A door closed; a door which shut off voices, wavering lights, the sombre shapes and the terrible watching eyes. The door which consigned her to death.

ONE

In every human life there are days of special importance, although we do not always recognise the significance of them until long after they have passed.

So it was with me, when I arrived in the village of Winterhill one afternoon late in September, 1886. I had spent the previous few days with friends, saying good-bye to them before they left for India, and had taken the train to Shottley Station, some five miles from the village.

I enjoyed the journey, drinking in the serene English countryside which I hadn't seen for some time, trying not to laugh at the self-importance of the station-master in his gold-braided uniform, as ceremoniously he led me to the gig which had come to collect me.

My heavy baggage had gone ahead, with Nan Ponsonby, my maid, and Barbara Wycombe, my companion, both of whom had gone to Winterhill the day before.

I thought it was a waste that I should have a paid companion, particularly as she was a girl I didn't care for much, but that was the price I had to pay to return to my native land.

Four years before, when my father had died, Lucia, my lovely, Italian-born mother, had returned to Florence. My father had been rich; my mother was richer still. We lived in a villa in which a prince would not have been ashamed to reside, surrounded by frescoed walls, marble pillars, priceless works of art and a veritable army of servants.

· But I missed England. The warm sun of Tuscany and the beauty of the villa and its formal gardens were no com-

pensation for green fields, mist lying on gentle hilltops, soft
rain and my own people. Thus, when I learned that my
great-aunt, Lucinda Oakley, who had died six months before,
had left me her house, Lucy's Cottage, in Lincolnshire, I had
given my poor mother no peace.

Finally, I suspect in sheer desperation, she had given way,
but only on condition that Nan went with me, and Babs, as
we called her, should be engaged to accompany me. She was
the daughter of an impoverished clergyman with seven other
offspring to contend with. His shabby rectory had been a mile
or so away from my father's home, and Lucia, whose heart
was as large as it was unwise, had taken the vicar's daughter
under her wing. She and I were six years old at the time.
Babs had played at Warren Lodge with me; eaten the ample
meals our cook had provided; been given my clothes, of
which I always had too many, and was the recipient of
generous presents on birthdays and at Christmas.

Even when we had left England, Lucia hadn't forgotten
her, and each year sent money so that Babs could have a
holiday with us. It so happened that she was at the villa when
at last Lucia's resistance had been worn down, and so was
at hand to become part of my mother's arrangements.

The gig waiting for me was driven by an old man called
Abe Benson. As we went on our leisurely way, he confided
in me that he had given up regular driving, but now and
then he obliged the local gentry by picking up a visitor from
the station, or delivering a parcel to the adjoining hamlet of
Little Firsk.

Having given me his reasons for collecting me, he lapsed
into silence and I was free to drink in the peace of the
meadows and hedgerows wearing the rich, ripe hues of
autumn. I didn't want to miss anything. I was like a miser,
storing it all in my memory, so that, when I returned to Italy
in six months time, I should be able to take out the various
sights, like choosing pictures from an album, and relive the
pleasure of being home again.

I don't know why I suddenly began to think of the dream
I had had the night before. Certainly it wasn't evoked by the

placid cows gazing benevolently at me on each side, nor the sight of sturdy men working in the fields, sleeves rolled up, arms burnt brown by sun and wind.

I didn't normally dream, or, if I did, I never remembered it when I awoke, but the nightmare had been so fearful that I could recall it as vividly as if it were still going on.

I had been in a room. The walls had been dark, the one behind a four-poster bed being panelled in wood. There had been heavy drapes at the window, a dull carpet beneath my feet, and a bedspread as black as a pall.

I had walked to the end of the bed and knew at once that there was someone in the room with me. I couldn't see them, but I could hear their breathing, even their heart-beat. The terror had exploded when I felt hands on me, propelling me towards the panelling. I had known, without a shadow of a doubt, that if I reached that wall I should die.

I had woken with a violent start, my pulse unsteady, thankful to find that I was in the McAllister's guest-room and that in half an hour or so their maid, Millicent, would be bringing me morning tea.

I pushed the dream aside, because it still made me nervous, and prodded Abe into conversation again.

" Do you know my house, Lucy's Cottage? It was left to me by my great-aunt."

He took so long to answer that I thought he'd fallen asleep and that his aged horse was finding its own way home, but finally he grunted.

" Aye, everyone knows Lucy's Cottage."

" What is it like? Is it small? How many rooms are there?"

" Never been inside. Wouldn't get me into that 'ouse, no matter what."

" Oh?" I was taken aback. My inheritance didn't sound too promising. " Why, what is wrong with it?"

" You'll see soon enough." He hunched his shoulders, warning me I'd get no more out of him. " Aye, you'll see."

I was glad when we reached our destination, very relieved

to find that Lucy's Cottage wasn't a derelict hovel, as I'd begun to fear, but an old, solidly-built house, with ivy growing profusely on the thick walls, with tiny windows, and a stout door, clad with iron straps and a business-like knocker.

The maid who admitted me was stocky and unkempt, with brownish hair growing low on her forehead, giving her a brooding look. The pale eyes and thin lips were far from welcoming, but I smiled warily and tried to make a good start.

"I'm Alexandra Leith; you're expecting me, of course. And you?"

"Kipps, Miss."

"What is your first name?"

"Dulcie."

Whatever else Kipps was, she wasn't a chatterbox, but before I could coax another word or two out of her Nan was there, kissing me soundly on both cheeks.

Nan had been my nurse and she still looked after me as if I were a baby, a state of affairs a trifle irksome at times. Not tall, but nicely rounded, she had white hair, always neatly wound into a flat bun on top of her head, and merry grey eyes.

"Welcome to Lucy's Cottage, love," she said, giving me a hug. "Did you have a good journey?"

"Yes, thank you. What's it like, my new home? I'm longing to see it all. It's much bigger than I imagined."

"Aye." Nan was leading me to the sitting-room. "It is that. Three rooms down here, apart from kitchen and so forth, and four bedrooms upstairs. There's a sort of back extension too; place for the maids, and the boxes and trunks."

"Oh, I like this."

We had reached the sitting-room by then and I was entranced by the homeliness of it. Chintz at the window and covering the comfortable settee and armchairs; a good plain carpet; yellow walls and a few rather awful paintings of horses. There was a small collection of fine pieces of porcelain, safely shut away in a glass-fronted corner cupboard but apart from a few silver ornaments on an occasional table by the fireplace the room was uncluttered and restful. Anything less like my mother's villa would have been hard to find. I hadn't seen Aunt Lucy since I was two years old, and consequently had no recollection of her, but I thought I knew what sort of person she must have been by the way she had furnished the room.

" Yes, I really do like it. Where's Babs?"

" Doing her hair for the twentieth time today, I shouldn't wonder."

Nan had never liked Babs.

" Is she settled in?"

" As if she owned the place." Nan was sour. " Never seen her so excited about anything; like she's bewitched. Keeps saying she would die of happiness if it were hers, but that's just like her. Always asking for things, and you and your mother are far too generous."

I tried to be fair.

" She hasn't had much."

" Neither have lots of others, but they don't keep cadging like she does. You want to stop giving her things, Miss Alex. She'd have the diamonds out of your rings if you gave her half a chance."

" Oh, Nan!"

" It's true, and you know it, and another thing . . ."

I didn't have time to find out what else Nan had to say, for Babs was there, coming forward to give me a peck on the cheek.

Against the dictates of fashion, Babs wore her hair in fat ringlets, the colour of corn, pulled back by a ribbon. Her eyes were blue and round, her cheeks pink and somehow shiny. She had always reminded me of a doll which I'd been given when I was a child. I'd hated the thing, because I thought it so much prettier than I was.

I chided myself, not for the first time, and tried to make amends for unkind thoughts.

" How nice you look, Babs!"

It wasn't really a lie, and Babs normally thrived on compliments. However, this particular one hardened her expression and made the full red lips thin ominously.

" Yes, it's a lovely dress, isn't it? It's one of yours, but of course you know that."

" It looks better on you," I said hastily, thankful when Kipps interrupted us with the tea. " Thank you, Dulcie. Miss Wycombe will pour."

I watched Babs's plump little hands on the silver milk-jug, wondering what I could say to lift the cloud, but I didn't have to bother, for she raised her head, her previous sullenness quite gone.

" This is a marvellous house, Alex." She said it as if she had fallen in love; almost breathless, with a thread of excitement woven into the words. " Wait till you see it. We only got here yesterday, but I've explored every bit of it, even the dairy at the back, and Dulcie has told me so much about it."

I gave Nan a quick look. She was clearly annoyed, but I pretended not to notice.

" I thought I saw a wood lying behind the house, down an embankment."

" Yes, you did." Babs handed me my cup. " That's Farthing Wood. You'd better not go there though."

" Why not? What's wrong with it?"

" The girl says it's haunted, like this house."

I felt an unexpected jolt, hardly hearing Nan's quick rebuke.

" Haunted? This house? Surely it can't be. I expect Kipps was making it up to frighten you."

" I'm sure she wasn't."

Babs was busy with wafer-thin sandwiches. Short of food as a child, unless she was with us, she had never got over her greediness, and it was no wonder that her curves were rather too ample for a twenty-one-year-old.

" She was quite serious. There are too many stories about it, and none of the villagers will come here. By the way, did you know the cook is deaf and dumb?"

It was another small shock, and I tore my gaze away from Babs, stuffing her mouth full, and turned to Nan again.

" That's right." Nan was short. " Sheena's her name, and she's getting on a bit, but she knows her job. Doesn't matter that she can't gossip all day long, like some."

Seeing that her acid comment was wasted on Babs, Nan took herself off, saying she was going to see that things were all right in the kitchen, and I was left with Babs.

She wasted no time, reaching for a slice of cake.

" Your aunt never left this house, at least, not in the last two years. Dulcie said she didn't set foot outside; she was afraid of offending whatever it is that's here."

" What utter nonsense! "

" No it isn't." Babs wasn't vexed at my rejection, because she could see I was growing uneasy. She liked to put other people out of countenance whenever she could. " She was made to stay here. The girl also told me that your great-aunt was scared of the wood; said it was an evil place. The villagers agree with her; they don't go there either."

" Well, I think it's rubbish." I tried to sound as though I meant it, but I knew Babs had a quick ear. " I don't believe it."

" Maybe you will, when you've been here a while." The glint of satisfaction faded and another emotion tinged her rather high-pitched voice. " Alex, I do so love it; this cottage I mean. I know we've only just arrived, but already I feel as if it were part of me. If it were mine, I should die of happiness."

Nan had been right and my disquiet increased. It really did sound as though Babs were bewitched. I tried to make light of it.

" Well, if you like it so much, perhaps I'll leave it to you when I die."

She stopped eating.

" But you won't die for ages."

" I hope not." My forced laugh wasn't very successful. " But one never knows."

" No, that's true." She was thoughtful. " Some people die quite young, don't they?"

" Yes, but I hope I shan't."

I wish I'd never started the conversation, but Babs wouldn't let it drop.

"But you'll keep your promise?"

"Promise?" There was a note of demand in Babs which I didn't like. "What promise?"

"The one you've just made. You will leave me the cottage when you die, won't you?"

There was a brief silence, but I was determined not to let it become a source of fear. It didn't matter either that I was agreeing to give my inheritance to a girl I didn't like, because I should live for years and years: death was a long way off.

"Yes, of course." I was very off-hand. "Lucy's Cottage will be yours, when I'm gone."

*   *   *

After tea, Babs showed me over the house with a proprietary air. Sheena Quinny was a poor old thing, shabby and nervous as she bobbed to me, but under wrinkled skin her bones were still good, her eyes almost luminous. I thought that she must have been quite lovely when she was young. If Lucia had been there, she would at once have found a way of communicating with the cook, but I could only smile sympathetically and admire the cleanliness of the kitchen.

My room, which had been Aunt Lucinda's, was left until last. Babs went in, leaving me to follow.

I felt as if I'd been hit hard over the heart and for a second or two I couldn't get my breath.

The room was that in my dream, exact in every detail. There was the four-poster, its cover not quite black but darkest blackberry hue; the panelled wall; the heavy curtains; deep mulberry carpet on the floor. It had no frills or furbelows; a very masculine room for a woman whom my mother had once described as a lacy butterfly.

I knew I was shaking, and hoped that Babs wouldn't notice. Fortunately, she had other things on her mind.

"We've got a lot of nice neighbours," she was saying,

when I had recovered sufficiently to listen to her. " Well-to-do, Dulcie says, and they've been calling here regularly since your aunt died, just to make sure that the servants were doing their work properly. Miss Oakley's solicitor asked them to do so. It was kind of them, wasn't it?"

I nodded, but I could see now why Kipps looked so disagreeable. She was probably heartily sick of unwanted supervision.

" I expect they'll invite us to dine with them." Babs's tone changed to one which I knew of old. " Of course, they'll think me a positive drab. You're so lucky, Alex, for your clothes are marvellous. That outfit's new, isn't it?"

I could see my reflection in the dressing-table mirror; light grey gown of watered silk, with the fashionably tight skirt, ending in a train; an embroidered jacket buttoned up to the throat.

" Yes, it is."

" It must have been terribly expensive." The envy was sharper now. " I've got simply nothing to wear, and if we do go out . . ."

I stopped it there and then, because I wanted to be alone to think.

" There's an evening-dress I don't care for much. It's never been worn. Lilac satin; it's in the wardrobe, I expect."

I watched her avaricious fingers plunging amongst my possessions, trying not to care.

" This one?" She turned, face radiant, the Paris gown draped over her arm. " Oh, do say it's this one, for it's perfect!"

" Yes, that one."

" May I go and start altering it? You don't need me for a while, do you?"

I shook my head, thankful when she was gone. I was never entirely at ease when I was with Babs. She made me defensive, as if I had to protect myself against her.

When I sat down and looked at myself in the mirror again, it was as if I were studying a stranger. Hair like a raven's wing, piled up in knot at the back of my head; eyes dark as night. Lucia always said my small nose and mouth were perfect, but she was prejudiced, and had I always been as pale as this?

I stayed there for another moment, but then I began to have a feeling that if I didn't move I should see more than myself in the looking-glass. I got up quickly, knowing I couldn't remain a second longer. It would be quite easy to ask Nan to put me into one of the other bedrooms, but I refused to give way to such weakness.

On the way to the door, there were goose-pimples on my arms, and I turned abruptly, certain that there was someone behind me. Of course there wasn't. That dream had really upset me and it was a quite remarkable coincidence that Lucinda's bedroom was so like the one in my nightmare.

But that's all it was; a coincidence. I thrust the whole thing to the back of my mind as I went downstairs to see what Sheena was preparing for the evening meal.

I wasn't going to let a dream spoil the happiness of my home-coming.

*   *   *

The next day, I went for a walk in Farthing Wood. Nan had put her feet up after lunch, as she always did, and Babs had gone to her room to finish altering her new dress.

It was really a challenge, rather than a desire to visit the place, which made me go. It was too stupid to admit that one was afraid of trees and bushes, and the small animals one would expect to find there.

From the gate of my garden, a narrow path wandered lazily down a bank and over a trickling stream.

I paused. The wood looked as if it were a live thing, lying there darkly; waiting. Even from that distance, I could understand how it had got its reputation, but I wasn't going to turn back now.

I went in, full of firm resolutions, treading on a carpet of leaves, gold, and brown, and palish green, watching the sun dapple through the shorn branches.

It ought to have reminded me of the wood near my old home, but it didn't. Cressy Wood, in autumn, had been a place of joy and my father and I had walked for hours in companionable silence, just happy to be together, surrounded by beauty. My thoughts winged back to those years, sad, because they were over, and I still missed my father so much. After our walks, we would return to Warren Lodge, tired but contented, shedding muddy boots and joining Lucia by the drawing-room fire. I could almost smell the sweet apple-wood logs burning in the grate; taste the hot buttered muffins and tea served in cups so thin one could almost see through them.

But the past was over and I was back in the rather un-certain present. I had gone some way by then and it was nothing like my childhood walks. It was a maze, crowding in on one, and I couldn't hear a sound. No birds were sing-ing and there wasn't a glimpse of a squirrel or a rabbit. It was a dead place and cold as a grave.

Dulcie's words had some meaning now. An evil place, where villagers wouldn't go and which Aunt Lucinda had feared. I was beginning to fear it too, but at first I was too proud to show it. I walked on, refusing to believe that it was growing darker. How could it be; my fob-watch assured me that it was only three o'clock?

It was then that I knew I wasn't alone. I swung round, expecting to see a poacher, or perhaps an unexpectedly bold villager, but there was no one. Nothing to see, except timber, and a tangle of shrubs and bushes matted together like barriers.

I didn't pretend any longer. I began to run as fast as I could, gasping when thorns caught at my skirt, as if they didn't want me to go.

I was heartily thankful when I saw the stream and grassy incline.

"Alexandra Leith, you're a fool," I said crossly as I reached the garden gate. "Just for that, you'll go again tomorrow."

My father would have been ashamed of me, for he had

always told me never to run away from anything which frightened me. "Stand up to it," he would say, "and then it cannot hurt you."

I was near the lavender-bushes growing by the back door when I heard the whisper. It wasn't an ordinary whisper, like a person speaking quietly under their breath, nor could I tell whether it was a man or a woman. It was just a suspicion of sound; almost an illusion. Yet despite the strange quality it was clear and penetrating.

"You need not have been afraid. I was there to look after you."

Fortunately, common sense came to my aid. I'd been thinking of my father, and it was the kind of reassurance he would have given me, had he been alive. It was simply a trick of the mind; remembering how he had loved and cared for me.

How could it possibly be anything else? No one had followed me out of Farthing Wood.

*   *   *

"Do you like it?"

Babs was pirouetting on the landing when I got upstairs, the satin material clinging to her like a second skin, and surely the neckline had not been so low when I bought the gown?

"Yes, you look charming."

It wasn't true; somehow Babs made the dress look common, but she lapped up my words.

"Now, you mustn't flatter me too much. It wouldn't do for you to turn a servant's head."

Hot irritation flooded through me. Babs was goading again.

"You're not a servant; you're my companion."

"Very much the same thing." A second's resentment, then the pleasure of her new possession washed it away. "Yes, it does suit me, doesn't it? I looked for you earlier, but you weren't in your room."

"No, I went for a walk in Farthing Wood."

She was speculative, concentrating on me as if she guessed that all was not well.

"Darling, how brave of you! Was there anything there?"

"Nothing, except the trees, of course."

She knew that I wasn't telling the truth, and her laugh was soft and malicious.

"An evil place. Don't forget, Alex; haunted, like this cottage. It's so exciting! I've always wanted to live in a house which is possessed."

"There's nothing wrong with the cottage." I was emphatic. "It's just silly rumours."

"Perhaps." She sighed. "Anyway, it's a wonderful place, and to think that one day it will be mine."

I was speechless as I left her. It was as if she were willing me to die, so that she could become mistress of Lucy's Cottage.

I ought to have been angry, but I wasn't. The emotion was nearer to fear, because there was an unnatural intensity about Babs' hunger. I had grown used to her wanting my clothes, trinkets and other small things. This was different.

I looked round the room, sensing that it had been waiting for me. I thought I heard a sigh of satisfaction, as if it were glad I'd come back, but I forced myself to be rational. The temptation to call Kipps and order her to move my possessions to another room was strong for a second or two; then I shook my head.

I tried to tell myself that I was being sensible; not letting absurd tales drive me out, but deep inside I knew it was more than that.

The feeling of exhaustion came over me suddenly, as if I had been running for miles, instead of the brief time it had taken me to get clear of the wood. I didn't even stop to undress, lying down and closing my eyes.

Then I was at the foot of the bed again, an unseen person close to me. The paralysing feeling of terror was back, and I was being pushed towards the panelling. I tried to scream aloud in my nightmare, but I knew that no sound was coming. Another foot or two and it would be over.

I jerked awake, brow damp, trembling all over. When I got to the dressing-table, I was shocked by what I saw. No colour in my cheeks or lips; eyes scared.

I tidied my hair, rubbing on a hint of rouge so that Nan's sharp eyes wouldn't notice any difference in me.

My hand was on the door-knob when it started. I was wide-awake, and quite alone, yet there was the sound of heavy, uneven breathing very close by.

I almost ran downstairs, pausing in the hall for a moment to regain my self-control. Then I went into the sitting-room where Nan was waiting to pour the tea.

Nan, but not Babs. Where had Babs been when I had stood petrified in Aunt Lucinda's bedroom?

TWO

Two days later, I received an invitation from Colonel and Mrs Max Mortimer to dine with them on Saturday. " It is my birthday," Athene Mortimer had written. "Do come, and bring Miss Wycombe with you. It will be such a good opportunity for you to meet your neighbours, for they will all be here."

" It hasn't taken long for our arrival to be noted." I gave my letter of acceptance to Nan. " Ask Dulcie to take this over to Chartley, will you? The house isn't too far away, is it?"

" No, other end of the village, a bit ways out. And you can be sure they know everything about you, Miss Babs, and me by now. In this sort of place, newcomers are fair game. Not much else to talk about, you see."

Later, I came across Kipps dusting the hall table and chairs.

" Shouldn't that have been done earlier? It's four o'clock."

" It were, Miss." Dulcie was like a thunder cloud. " Miss Nan said it weren't right and 'ad to be done over. Only just found time. She thinks I've got six pairs of 'ands, that one."

" That will do." I squashed the rebellion straight away. " Miss Ponsonby is quite correct. Work should be done well, whatever it is. Did you take my note to Mrs Mortimer?"

" Aye." The corners of the maid's mouth turned upwards, ill humour over. " 'Spect they'll all want to know what you've seen since you got 'ere."

" Seen?" I stopped at the foot of the stairs. " What do you mean? What sort of things?"

"Whatever things Miss Oakley saw." Kipps was smugly satisfied; my attention was engaged. "No one thought any-one would come to Lucy's Cottage again, not after . . ."

"After what?" I was sharp. "For goodness' sake, what are you trying to say? If you mean that this house is haunted, I simply don't believe it, nor do I think my aunt was too afraid to leave it. She probably just didn't want to go out."

"No, it weren't like that." The duster was stilled, one foot rubbing against the other leg. "She were feared right enough. Said as much to me one day."

"What exactly did she say?"

"That 'er 'ome was a prison. It wouldn't let 'er go. She couldn't offend."

"What wouldn't? Really, you are too exasperating with your half-hints and innuendoes. Who couldn't she offend?"

"Don't know what them are; innu . . . what you said. But I do know there's summat in this 'ouse. I feels it now and then, but it's not after me. Don't own the place, see? You'll feel it, soon enough."

"What will I feel? If you don't give me a straight answer, I swear I shall be really vexed with you. What am I likely to feel?"

"That something's 'ere with you. You won't see nothin', I don't suppose, but you'll know right enough." The smile was gloating. "It's in the wood too. 'Orrible place that. Wouldn't catch me goin' there."

My hand was tighter on the newel-post. I was remembering what I had felt in my bedroom, and the sensation of a presence near to me when I had been in Farthing Wood. I ought to have sent the abominable Kipps packing, but there were still questions to be answered.

"I understand some of the ladies who live round here came to see you after Miss Oakley died. Did they notice anything?"

"Oh them!" Dulcie almost spat it out. "They didn't notice nothin' but dust, which weren't there anyway."

"And Sheena?"

Kipps shrugged.

"Don't know. She can't say, can she? I think she's a bit funny in the 'ead meself. Perhaps she feels summat, perhaps she don't."

"I'll see her later."

"Won't get you nowhere." Kipps started to polish again. "Maybe you'd better sell the 'ouse to Colonel Mortimer. Always wanted it, 'e 'as, but yer aunt wouldn't part with it. Kept on to 'er; offered 'er a good price, I 'eard."

"Colonel Mortimer?" I frowned. "Why should he want Lucy's Cottage?"

"Don't know, Miss, never asked 'im."

I knew I wouldn't get any more out of Dulcie and so I went on my way, the feeling of worry increasing. Babs wanted the house with a depth of passion she had never shown before; now I learned that Colonel Mortimer had wanted it too. What was it about the place which attracted everyone so? I wasn't sure that I even liked it myself. My first pleasure had long since died away. I chided myself again for being a fool and put the matter out of my mind.

On Saturday evening, when I was almost ready, Babs appeared. She looked at my white silk with the square décolletage, short puffed sleeves, and tiny seed pearls trimming the train of the skirt.

"How splendid you look!" Babs had on the lilac gown and she had arranged her hair in a bun on the crown of her head, with a fringe crimped tightly with curling tongs. "You are positively stunning, and those pearls. . . ."

I steeled myself to refuse what was coming. Babs only praised my appearance when she wanted something.

"It does make a difference, having jewellery like yours. Even the humblest dress can look magnificent. I wondered if you would choose pearls, or the amethysts. Such a wonderful colour, amethysts. I really do believe that they are my favourites."

So that was it. She wanted the necklace and earrings left to me by my grandmother. Well, for once I would listen to Nan.

"Yes, they're pretty enough."

There was a silence, Babs's smile becoming a trifle fixed.
I wasn't responding.

" Of course, I've nothing like that to wear, and this neck
does seem rather . . . well . . . bare."

" Perhaps you shouldn't have cut so much away. What
about the silver locket I gave you? Wouldn't that suit?"

Babs's laugh was brief and harsh.

" My dear, certainly not; far too small. Don't think I
wasn't grateful for it. I'm always grateful, as you know, for
any crumbs which come my way, but it wouldn't be right for
this dress."

I kept quiet, watching the dislike in Babs's eyes reflected
in the mirror. She wasn't done yet and I knew it; Babs never
gave up. She'd accepted that her first choice wasn't forth-
coming, but now she was considering an alternative.

" Gold chains might do." She moved nearer, so that she
was looking over my shoulder. Yellow locks close to black
ones; azure eyes fixed determinedly on mine. " But, of
course, I haven't got those either."

I gave in. It was childish to begrudge so small a thing and,
in any event, the atmosphere would be uncomfortable for
days if Babs didn't get her own way.

As I got my jewel-box out, a nervous thought ran through
my mind. Would Babs be as determined about Lucy's Cottage
as she had been about the amethysts?

" They belonged to my grandmother," I said without
expression. " I can't give them away, but please wear them
tonight."

" Dearest, how kind you are! You do spoil me so, and
I'll be very careful with them."

Eager fingers did up the clasp, all chagrin gone.

" Ask Nan to come and see me, will you, Babs?"

" Of course, dear, I'll go straight away. I feel so grand
now, and I shan't disgrace you at the Mortimers. I wouldn't
want them to think that you had a poor, dowdy companion."

When she was gone, I put the box away. Nan was right;
I was foolish to keep giving in to Babs, but she was so

persistent. I was slipping on a gold bracelet when I heard
Nan come in.

"Good heavens, Nan, you've been quick. I didn't want
you to run all the way. I just wanted to say . . ."

I looked round, finding it hard to swallow.

There was no one there. Not Nan; not Babs; no one. Yet
I was quite certain that someone had come in. The physical
presence of another person in the room had been too strong
for me to have been mistaken.

When the door opened, I went back to the mirror, pretending to make a last-minute adjustment to my hair. I didn't
want Nan to ask questions which I couldn't answer.

Kipps was on the landing, looking sly. I said shortly:

"Dulcie, did you come into my room just now?"

"No." She was full of injured innocence. "Came up
behind Miss Ponsonby, didn't I?"

"Yes." Nan was beginning to frown; she always knew
when I was worried. "Yes, you did. What's wrong, Miss
Alex? You seem . . ."

"It's nothing; nothing at all. Is Benson here with that gig
of his?"

"At the door and waiting, and here's Miss Babs, ready
too."

I nearly asked Babs if she'd come back into my room and
then left quickly before I could see her, but it would have
sounded so ridiculous.

As I started down the stairs, following Babs and Nan,
Kipps grinned, keeping her voice low, so that the others
shouldn't hear her.

"Said so, didn't I? I knew it 'ud come."

*   *   *

Babs and I were greeted warmly by Max Mortimer. He
looked the typical country squire, and so English that I could
have hugged him. Tall, well-built, with ruddy cheeks and a
neat beard and moustache turning grey, he was exactly what
I had hoped for as a neighbour. I liked the twinkle in his

light brown eyes; it was the same look that I had seen in my father so often.

" This is my wife, Athene."

Athene was younger than the colonel; about forty, I judged. Her red hair was slipping from its pins, but it was thick and glossy like satin. Her clothes were unfashionable and of garish colour, yet her thin, angular frame was elegant and the long, slanting green eyes instantly attractive.

" I'll take you round to meet the others." Her voice was low and husky, almost seductive in its quality. " Max, you look after Miss Wycombe."

I was introduced to Dr Carlton, so nondescript that he slipped from the mind almost as soon as we left him.

" If you must be ill, keep it simple," advised Athene. " I don't think George is up to much more than measles or childbirth. Fortunately, we're all terribly healthy here; it must be the air."

" Where does he live, just in case?"

" At The Ridge. He's got a housekeeper named Merryweather, who drinks like a fish, and the two maids, Maud and Kitty, could teach a Parisian whore a thing or two."

I laughed and Athene gave a faint sigh.

" Thank God to find a woman who doesn't have the vapours whenever I open my mouth. I'm rather blunt, I fear. After all, what's the point of wrapping up the truth so one can't recognise it? Now, this is our rector."

The Rev. Postumus Dauber looked undernourished and rather ill-tempered, and we moved on as soon as we could.

" Poor devil." Athene shook her head, making her earrings jangle fiercely. " The rectory's a pigsty, and no wonder. Meg Clapcott, his maid-of-all-work, is a slut. I don't think she's all there myself. Ah, Gavin, darling."

I looked quickly at Mrs Mortimer. The crisp tone used to censure her guests' servants had gone completely. Her voice was soft, full of love; her smile as gentle as a kiss.

" Our son, Gavin. Dearest, this is Miss Leith, who's come to live at Lucy's Cottage."

Gavin took my hand, raising it to his lips, giving me a

second or two to study him. Chestnut curls, pale brown eyes like his father's, clean bones and a good tailor. Gavin Mortimer was a remarkably attractive creature and it was no wonder that his mother adored him.

" I was told the new owner was comely." He kept my hand in his. " Nobody told me she was a beauty."

I almost blushed, even though I had had my fair share of flattery. There was a hint of intimacy in the words which was delightfully dangerous.

" Mayn't I keep her, Athene? Do you have to drag her away?"

" Yes, I do. Miss Leith hasn't met the Baxters yet, nor Nadine and Felix."

" Have you put her next to me at table?"

" As a matter of a fact I have. Now, Gavin . . ."

" You're so clever, sweetheart." He kissed his mother's cheek and winked at me. " Don't let Gillian talk you into helping her. I can think of far more interesting things for you to do."

" Gillian?"

We went on our way and I was quite sorry to see Gavin go.

" Gillian Baxter. She feels her mission in life is to do good works, like taking home-made soup to the poor in the village and knitting garments which don't fit anyone. I didn't like to tell her that, the other day, old Mrs Prinne said her broth tasted like stale cabbage-water. Fortunately, I had my brandy-flask with me and a drop or two of that improved it no end."

Clearly, Athene was an unusual woman.

We duly met the Baxters, he a retired solicitor, keen on gardening, and busy little Gillian, who eyed me thoughtfully, as if she saw new raw material at hand.

Nadine Lancaster was quite a different proposition. Russet hair, low on the nape of her neck, skin like milk, violet eyes, and a suspicion of a double chin which gave her age away. She was meticulously groomed, expensively dressed and very much aware of her mature charms, welcoming me rather distantly and nodding in the direction of Felix Lancaster, her blond and good-looking nephew.

The last guest was Geoffrey Thatcher, a grey man, with eyes and hair the colour of steel. He seemed withdrawn and almost lifeless and certainly not enjoying Athene's birthday party.

"Rather a stick-in-the-mud," said Athene when we were out of ear-shot, "but nice enough. Owns Bromwell, that house up on the hill. Just as well he's got money; the place has twenty rooms and the garden goes on for ever."

Finally, we were all seated at table, Gavin smiling at me in satisfaction. The colonel's valet, Gideon Woodbyrne, was doubling as butler, so Gavin said under his breath, and there were two smartly-dressed maids fluttering round us to serve Flemish soup; turbot; red mullet and Italian sauce; veal and truffles; lamb cutlets with a piquante sauce; braised ham, and grouse pie.

I had quite forgotten how much the English ate. At home, Lucia and I ate simply, almost frugally. My appetite was small and Lucia was always thinking about her perfect, hour-glass figure and what too much good living would do to it.

I had to refuse plum tart with whipped cream, punch jelly, ices, and the marrow pudding which followed, hoping Athene wouldn't think me pernickety or ungrateful.

I saw the colonel turn to speak to Gavin. It was not only Athene who doted; Max's expression was eloquent in its reflection of love and pride in his only child.

The talk was general during the main part of the meal. Felix had been placed next to Babs and he was being very attentive. I was thankful, for Babs was always easier to handle when a personable young man showed interest in her.

It was when the dessert was being served that the conversation changed from inconsequences to a more serious subject. We had a choice of almonds and raisins in a silver dish; chocolates piled high on a plate, and red-cheeked apples arranged in a mound, evergreen leaves between each layer.

" Is there any news of poor Ruth?'

Max raised his head, glancing in the direction of Gillian Baxter.

" I'm afraid not." He was regretful, peeling an apple with neat precision. "Not a trace of her, in spite of all the searches which have been made."

" How awful!" Gillian's eyes were moist. " She was such a nice child; I simply can't stop thinking about her. I really do feel that her brother was wrong to leave her alone at The Hall."

" Hardly alone." Max gave a faint smile. " Sir Richard has a host of servants, including a companion for his sister."

" That's not the same thing; you know what I meant. Servants aren't the same as family."

I caught an odd glance exchanged between the colonel and Woodbyrne as the latter bent to pass chocolates to Nadine Lancaster. I was trying to interpret it, when Nadine said briskly:

" Silly chit, I've no sympathy with her. She ran away from a perfectly good home." She savoured a lemon cream, touching her lips daintily with her napkin. "What else could have happened?"

" Almost anything these days." Dr Carlton was gloomy. " One does hear of such dreadful occurrences."

" Not here in Winterhill." Mrs Baxter was quick to deny such a possibility. " Not to Ruth Segrave."

When no one spoke, I took advantage of the pause.

" I do hope that you won't think me inquisitive, but who is Ruth Segrave, and what has become of her?"

" She's Richard Segrave's young sister." Max dipped into the crystal finger-bowl. " Their father lives in Switzerland; an invalid, I believe. Richard looks after the girl, at least, he did. As to what's become of her, that's the problem. We don't know."

" Has she been missing for long?"

" Since Thursday. No, I think it was Wednesday, wasn't it, Athene?"

" That's right." Athene's face had closed up, as if she didn't want to talk about the subject in front of strangers.

B

" The servants at The Hall saw her at dinner on Wednesday, so I'm told, but not after that."

" The day before I arrived." I was pensive, but curiously uneasy too, although I had no idea why. " Does Sir Richard know his sister is missing?"

Max was cooler too.

" A wire was sent to him, of course. As you'll have gathered from what Gillian said, he's away; touring Europe with a party of friends. A letter was sent too, to an hotel where it was thought he was staying, but since he hasn't returned I assume he is still in ignorance of what's happened."

" I see. What about the police?"

Everyone stared at me, even Babs, as if I had said something indecent, but I had to go on.

" Wouldn't it have been wise to tell them?"

" Not really our place." Mortimer was firm. " Richard will do that when he gets back."

" It might be too late."

Athene's laugh was artificial, like chips of ice against a glass.

" You speak as if she'd been abducted. It's nothing like that. Nadine's right; she ran away. Perhaps she went to a relative."

" She must have been very unhappy to leave such a lovely place as Winterhill. Why was she so distressed?"

" I've no idea." Athene's strong white teeth snapped an almond in half as if it had offended her. " She didn't confide in me. I shouldn't worry, Miss Leith. Her companion is writing to her aunt and cousins. She'll soon be found and her brother's bound to be back before long."

" Perhaps she was afraid of Farthing Wood."

I hadn't meant to say that. The words simply slipped out and I could feel disapproval thicken in the air.

" Why should she be?" Nadine was positively hostile. " What's wrong with Farthing Wood?"

" I don't know," I replied untruthfully, " but my maid, Dulcie, says it's haunted, and that my aunt hated it."

The tension relaxed at once and Athene was her ironic
self again.

"Ah, I see, that's it, is it? My dear, take no notice of what
that minx Kipps has to say. She's a mischief-maker and she's
bored. Most servants are and so they make up these ludicrous
tales to amuse themselves."

"She said that Aunt Lucinda never left the cottage at all."

I was grateful that the displeasure had lifted, but I wanted
to know what Athene and the others had to say about that.

"No, she didn't, towards the end." Max was kindly. "In
that, Kipps is right. Miss Oakley didn't go out, but it wasn't
because she disliked the wood."

"Dulcie said the cottage wouldn't let her go."

"There you are!" Athene was triumphant. "What did
I tell you? These gels are quite impossible. Ignore her."

"Athene's right." Max sighed. "It wasn't anything like
that. She had grown old and her bones ached; she just didn't
want to leave her home. That's so, George, isn't it?"

Carlton nodded.

"Yes, yes."

I turned my head to look at the doctor. There had been
something about the way he had answered which wasn't
right, but before I could probe any more Athene was leading
the ladies to the drawing-room, the men settling down to
their port and cigars.

When Athene came over to speak to me, I said ruefully:

"You must have thought me very rude. I didn't mean to
ask so many questions about Ruth Segrave, for it's none of
my business, but it was because of what Kipps had said. I
just wondered if . . ."

"Of course, of course." Athene waved a forgiving hand.
"Just like all these wenches. As I say, take no notice of her."

"She did tell me one other thing." I was cautious, but
Athene was smiling at me tranquilly and so I risked it. "It
may be another lie, but she said Colonel Mortimer had tried
to persuade my aunt to sell Lucy's Cottage to him."

"No, that's absolutely right. Max did try and so did I."

"But why do you want it?" I looked round the room,

furnished with impeccable taste and full of treasures. " You can't want to leave such a house as this."

Again the low chuckle, almost as deep as a man's.

" It wasn't for us; it was for Gavin. He wants his own place, and that's natural. We're afraid he might go away, perhaps to London. We thought if we could buy Lucy's Cottage for him, we could keep him near us. You see, I couldn't have another child, and Gavin is so precious to us. The thought of not seeing him from one month's end to another is quite unbearable." The smile was warmer as she asked hopefully: " I suppose you wouldn't let us buy it, would you? Gavin has always loved the cottage."

I was taken aback. The question had come so suddenly that I didn't have time to prepare a careful answer. I was just conscious that yet another person was captivated by my new home.

" I shouldn't have sprung it on you so abruptly." Athene dismissed the matter quickly. " Wait until you've been here a while, then think about it. You weren't proposing to live here for good, were you?"

" No, I shall be going back to Italy in a few months' time, but I don't really think I want to part with the cottage."

" We'll see. You may be quite glad to get rid of it by then."

I wondered why it sounded like a threat: then I brushed the idea aside. I was crediting Athene with thoughts which clearly she did not have. She and Max just wanted the cottage so that their beloved son would live near to them. I switched back to Ruth.

" Do you really think Ruth ran away?"

Athene was very close to me, but for a second it seemed as if she were miles away; remote, unreachable.

" I think so." She hesitated. " We don't talk about it, but since you're now one of us I suppose there's no harm in you knowing. If I don't tell you, somebody else will. Besides, you'll see then why enquiries as to her whereabouts have to be handled carefully. Ruth was not quite stable. Not mad, of course; nothing like that, but these very old families . . .

well . . . it does happen now and then. When Max said her
father was an invalid, he was being tactful. It's said he's in
some kind of sanatorium; kept out of the way, as it were.
His mind's gone, you see, and that's why Sir Richard has the
care of Ruth. Yes, I'm sure Nadine's right. Ruth ran away,
you can be sure of it."

"Really, Alex," said Babs a few minutes later. "How can
you pry so? Whatever will they think of us? We shan't get
asked anywhere if you behave like this."

"I don't need you to teach me my manners," I returned
coldly. "I think the disappearance of a young girl is important, even if you don't. Go and flirt with Felix Lancaster.
I'm sure that he'll see that you're invited to the next
party."

Babs's petulance melted at once and she was glowing with
inner satisfaction.

"Do you think so? Yes, he does seem to like me, doesn't
he? He's very good-looking, don't you think?"

"Yes, and here he comes."

As Babs moved away, her coffee-cup tilted, pouring brown
liquid all over my skirt. I knew that she'd done it on
purpose, but, of course, I could never make her admit it.

"Alex! I'm so sorry."

Her voice was full of contrition, but her eyes weren't. In
a trice, Athene was leading me to the door, giving one of
the maids instructions to take me to her bedroom and repair
the damage. When the stain was removed, the girl poured
water into a china bowl, so that I could rinse my fingers.

"Shall I stay, Miss?"

"No, that's not necessary, thank you. There's a lot for
you to do downstairs."

She beamed at the half-sovereign tucked into her hand,
and I glanced round my hostess's room. Cool, clear colours;
delicate period furniture, and a pencil sketch of Gavin over
the bed, drawn with love and sensitivity.

I had to turn a corner to reach the main landing, but,
before I could do so, I heard a woman's voice. It was low at
first, but so intense that it carried in the stillness.

" I must see you alone, you know I must! It's what you promised."

I couldn't hear what the man said, but I knew then that it was Nadine Lancaster and that she was growing more agitated.

I fled back to the bedroom, waiting a few minutes before venturing out again. When I reached the landing, Nadine and the unknown man had gone.

In the drawing-room, I looked at the men, trying to guess which of them had been upstairs a few minutes before, but I soon gave up. It was another thing which was none of my business.

" A penny for them."

I caught my breath and Gavin Mortimer pulled a face.

" Oh dear, now I've startled the life out of you, and I was determined to make a good impression on you."

" Were you?" I allowed him to lead me to a love-seat in one of the alcoves. " Why was that, Mr Mortimer?"

" So formal?" He was quizzical. " You'll have to call me Gavin sooner or later, so why not now? I shall certainly call you Alex. As to why I wanted to make a good impression, that was because I wanted to ask you to come riding with me."

" I haven't got a horse."

Suddenly, we both started to laugh at my ridiculous answer. Not a polite titter, but genuine amusement, easily shared.

" No, I don't suppose you brought one back from Italy in your luggage, but never mind, we've got plenty."

" Well . . ."

" If you're afraid of me, we could always take Miss Wycombe and Felix as chaperones."

" I'm not in the least afraid of you."

His smile was gone and he was taking in every line of my face.

" No, I'm sure you're not. You're like my mother; women of your sort are never afraid."

I wondered what Gavin would say if I told him how scared

I had been in my bedroom, and whilst I was in the wood.
This wasn't the time for such confessions; I should have to
wait until I knew him better. Meanwhile, I basked in un-
deserved praise.

" Thank you."

" And you'll come?"

" Yes."

" Soon?"

We were laughing again, not for any particular reason,
but simply because we liked each other.

" Very well; soon."

" Good, I'll call for you the day after tomorrow, at about
eleven o'clock. Do you enjoy living in Florence?"

" Most of the time. I get homesick now and then, and
that's why I was so pleased when my great-aunt left me
Lucy's cottage. It gave me an excuse to come back."

I almost asked how Gavin would like to be the owner of
my house, but just stopped myself in time. Probably he knew
nothing about his parents' plans, and they wouldn't thank
me for spoiling a surprise. I found myself thinking rather
differently about Athene's request. If I couldn't stay in
England, I thought I might like Gavin to have my cottage.

" There's a delightful sketch of you in your mother's
room," I said, leaving the matter of the cottage for the time
being. " Who is the artist?"

" Athene. She's very gifted."

I wasn't altogether surprised. There was far more than
technical perfection in the drawing. It was like a picture in
a shrine; an object of devotion.

" I'm glad you came."

Gavin broke into my thoughts and said it as if he meant
it. I had a strong premonition that, despite the fact that we
were in a room full of people, he was about to embrace me.

Then he gave a slow, lazy smile, leaning back.

" Yes, you were right, Alexandra Leith, I was going to
kiss you. You see, I can read your mind, as well as your
beauty, but perhaps this isn't the most appropriate of places."

I knew I was blushing, furious with myself because I

didn't want Gavin to think me unsophisticated. Usually, I had no trouble at all in dealing with amorous men, but Gavin was different. Everything in Winterhill seemed to me to be different.

"I'm sorry." He touched my hand lightly. "I've embarrassed you, and I didn't mean to do that. Forgive me?"

"Of course." I was anxious to change the topic of conversation, although the danger had passed. "Babs seems to find Felix Lancaster good company."

It wasn't a very happy choice of subject, for Gavin's face grew serious and all the banter had gone from his voice when he spoke.

"Have you known her long?"

"Since we were children."

"Mm."

"What does that mean?"

"She doesn't like you. She's jealous; did you know that?"

I was amazed. So much percipience in so short a time.

"Yes, I knew it, but how did you?"

"I saw her watching you at dinner. A poor man's daughter, I take it?"

"Yes, but I don't think we ought to . . ."

"No, of course not, but be careful."

"Of what?"

"Miss Wycombe. Jealousy is a dangerous thing."

He sounded so grim that I felt a flicker of nervousness, my mind racing back to things which had happened in the cottage.

"Babs wouldn't do anything to hurt me. She may be tiresome at times, but she wouldn't . . ."

The words died away in the depths of Gavin's eyes.

"You're not sure, are you?" he asked quietly. "Perhaps that's just as well. It'll keep you on your guard."

"You're trying to frighten me."

"No, but remember what I've said, and another thing."

"Yes?"

"I wouldn't go into Farthing Wood if I were you. Oh,

I know Kipps mustn't be taken too seriously, and I certainly don't believe all the old wives' tales told about the place, but it has got a bad reputation. It's no good pretending otherwise, because if you stay here you'll find out anyway."

" But Miss Lancaster said . . ."

" Nadine, yes."

I noticed that Gavin's mouth had become a straight line, and followed his gaze to where his father and Nadine were talking together.

" Well, she didn't want to scare you, and neither do I, but don't walk in the wood."

" I'm not afraid of trees."

It wasn't true, but I wanted to maintain his illusion that I was like his mother.

" It wasn't the trees I was talking about."

" Gavin, what . . ."

We had no more time, for Max and Geoffrey Thatcher had joined us, and the subject of that year's harvest swept aside Gavin's cautionary advice.

But when he said good night to me, holding my hand firmly in his, he said softly:

" Don't forget what I've said, Alex, will you? Keep out of Farthing Wood, and remember, too, that Barbara Wycombe is no friend of yours. She never will be."

THREE

Abe Benson drove Babs and me back to the cottage. Babs was full of Felix Lancaster, her eyes like stars. I made appropriate responses now and then, but I couldn't get Gavin's warning about her out of my mind.

I'd always known Babs was envious of me; even if we had had an equal share of this world's goods, she still wouldn't have liked me, but what Gavin was talking about was quite different. Surely Babs wouldn't . . .?

'To think that one day it will be mine.' That was what Babs had said of Lucy's Cottage. One day, when I was dead.

I forced myself to stop thinking of such things, only to find Gavin's second warning had slithered in to take the place of the first. 'Don't walk in Farthing Wood.'

I would have liked to have taken his advice, but I knew I couldn't. My father would have been disappointed in me for giving in so quickly. I would have to go again, if only to prove to myself that there was nothing wrong with the wood, or my hitherto robust spirit.

" Felix's aunt is giving a party soon. We're to be invited, isn't that marvellous?"

We were making our way upstairs by then, accompanied by Nan, who had waited up for us.

" Yes."

Babs looked over her shoulder, the pleasure vanishing as if wiped away by a cloth.

" You don't sound at all pleased. Don't you want me to meet people like Felix? Just because I'm your companion, it doesn't mean . . ."

" Oh, Babs!" I was tired, my thoughts thoroughly mixed

up. An argument with Babs was the last thing I needed. " Of course I want you to meet people . . . especially like Felix. I'm very pleased we're to be asked. Now do go to bed."

The sunny smile was back.

" That's all right then. I suppose I'll have to wear this dress again." The sigh was theatrical. " Everyone will recognise it, of course, but I haven't got anything else that's fit to be seen in."

" We'll talk about it tomorrow. Good night!" I waited until she had gone, knowing that Nan was about to give me a piece of her mind. " Nan, do go to bed, you must be dropping. I know I am, and I can easily manage."

" But . . ."

" I'd rather."

Nan's lips compressed. She didn't like being shut out, even in small ways.

" All right, if you say so, but don't let Miss Babs talk you into giving her your whole wardrobe. Let her wear the dress twice; other people have to."

" Yes, yes! Good night!"

I leaned against the closed door, thankful to be alone.

I wanted to think about Gavin, but only the bad things came into my mind. Jealous Babs; Farthing Wood.

As I undressed, my thoughts switched to Ruth Segrave. Not quite stable, Athene had said, but was that right? I had had the distinct impression that the Mortimers and their friends had been evasive on the subject of Ruth, but then I shrugged.

I was making a mountain out of a molehill. They had helped to look for her; sent a message to her brother. It was obviously useless to communicate with the girl's father. What else could they have done, and, as suggested, she could merely have gone away without telling anyone to visit a relative. Her companion would soon receive replies to her enquiries, and probably all would be well.

I was brushing my hair, too tired to think any more, when I heard it, and my hand froze in mid-air. There was no mistaking it. It was a moan; a low gasp of pain. I held my breath, waiting to see if I had been wrong, but then it came again. Dreadful to hear; a human being in agony.

I fled to the door, my cries bringing Nan, Babs and even Kipps rushing to the passage, candles held high.

"Miss Alex, Miss Alex, what is it?" Nan was holding my hand tightly. "Love, you're trembling all over. Whatever's wrong?"

Babs was clutching her dressing-gown tightly about her plump form, the wild-rose gone from her cheeks.

"Good heavens, I thought you were being murdered. You frightened the life out of me. What's the matter?"

Dulcie said nothing, her gaze fixed steadily on me. Part of my mind registered the fact that she was still dressed, although it was past midnight.

"In there . . . in my room." I was glad of Nan to hold on to. "In my room. There was a moan . . . someone was moaning."

Babs was less sure of herself and Kipps began to back away. She wasn't smug any more, but clearly nervous. Only Nan was calm and collected.

"Now, now, there's no need to be afraid. It must have been the wind, or something like that. There's no one else in your room, is there?"

"Come in and listen for yourselves." I was brittle, for I could see the disbelief on the faces lit by tiny flames which moved back and forth in the draught. "It wasn't my imagination; I know it wasn't. Come and hear."

They followed me in, Babs and Dulcie with some reluctance. The room looked just the same as I had left it, the shadows driven further into the corners by extra light. We all stood quite still for a long minute. Then Babs said testily:

"I can't hear a thing. Really, Alex, you . . ."

"There was a sound." I was still shaking, helpless because they wouldn't believe me. "It was a moan, I swear it was."

"The wind in the ivy outside, that'll be it, or maybe a creaking floorboard. Could be draught in the chimney too." Nan was leading me back to bed. "You know what these old places are like; all sorts of funny noises. Nothing now, is there? Come along, you lie down and get some sleep. You'll have forgotten all about it by the morning. Miss Babs, off you go. You too, girl. I want you up promptly at five-thirty, and there'll be no time for yawning when there's work to be done."

Nan shooed the others out and I lay very still. They hadn't believed a word I'd said. Babs had been scared and I'd caught a moment of real terror in Kipps, but that was only because my screams had startled them, my insistence on what I'd heard making their flesh creep.

Certainly nothing had happened whilst they'd been in the room, but I knew quite well that I hadn't been mistaken, and it was nothing to do with ivy or draught in the chimney.

It had been a human voice, muffled in pain, crying out in an empty room.

* * *

It was the next day that I noticed the portrait in the dining-room. I couldn't imagine why I hadn't seen it properly before, because it was so striking. Babs was sleeping late, and I was breakfasting alone, toying with food which I didn't want.

The man in the picture was so handsome that he almost took the breath away. The powdered wig; the painted face with its beauty spot; the richly-patterned brocade coat, and lace ruffles falling against slender hands. A man from another age, but as alive and vibrant as if he were sitting at the table with me.

I hadn't any idea why the painting made me nervous, but it did. When Dulcie came in to clear, I asked her if she knew who he was, but she had no idea. Just a man: a man with a flawless face, and eyes which followed one round the room.

I left the dining-room quickly. I really had to get a grip on myself. I had never before let such trivial things upset me: it was wholly foreign to my nature to hear noises and worry about paintings and trees.

That night, the moans came again. At first, I was determined not to call the others, but as the noise continued I could bear it no longer. When Nan and Babs arrived, there was nothing, and they were as disbelieving as before.

I was heavy-eyed when I put my riding-habit on the next morning. Gavin was due in half an hour and he would notice my pallor: he was very perceptive. I straightened up. This had to stop. I couldn't let nerves get the better of me. I had allowed stories of Lucy's Cottage and Farthing Wood to prey on my mind more than I had realised. I was ready to hear and see anything.

I picked up my gloves and whip, hoping Gavin would think my habit suited me. Severe, of course, but no less fetching for all that.

I was halfway across the floor when I stopped short. The smell hadn't been there a second ago; I was sure of it. A peculiar foetid odour, which I couldn't place.

"Nan!" I knew my voice wasn't quite steady as I went out into the corridor. "Nan, will you come here for a moment, please?"

Nan was in the linen press, sorting sheets, and came at once.

"Yes, Miss Alex, what is it?"

"Can you smell something?"

Nan gave me a wary look.

"No, can't say I can."

"But you must!" I knew my tone was rising. "I can still smell it. You must be able to!"

Nan patted my arm.

"Come down, there's a dear. Mr Mortimer will be here any minute. Perhaps we'd better move you to another room before tonight. Would you like that?"

"No!" I was angry, because I didn't want to be humoured. I wanted Nan to admit that she could detect the odour too. "No, I don't want to move. For heaven's sake, don't baby me. I'm not a child."

"No, no, of course not, and my sense of smell's not what it was."

I said nothing, feeling the screw of fear make another

turn inside me. Nan's sense of smell was very acute, but she
hadn't noticed anything in my room. Only I was aware of
whatever it was. Only I had heard the moaning.

I felt better after my ride. If Gavin saw anything different
about me, he hadn't said so. We had talked of horses, music,
poetry and Europe and, when he touched my hand as he
helped me to dismount, I hadn't minded at all.

I was changing for luncheon when I became aware of the
breathing again. My eyes looked back at me from the mirror
as I held my own breath. There was no mistake. The unsteady
gasping went on and I watched the colour drain from my face
until it was like a sheet. It only lasted for seconds, but it
seemed like hours.

Then it stopped and I found that my mouth was as dry as
dust. I hadn't intended to mention it to anyone else, but
when Nan came in with fresh towels I simply couldn't
prevent myself from blurting it out.

Nan looked grave.

"You're getting real fanciful, Miss Alex, and I'm that
worried about you. Moans, smells and now breathing.
Perhaps you should see Dr Carlton. Maybe a tonic would do
you good."

"Certainly not." I was short with her. "I'm not ill and
I don't want to see Dr Carlton. Why don't you believe me?
You know I don't lie."

"No, no, of course you don't, my lamb." Nan's warm
hand was over mine, strong and reassuring. "But you've not
been yourself lately. I think it's this house."

"I'm quite all right and there's nothing wrong with the
cottage."

Although I had just insisted that I never lied, I had to say
it. It would have sounded worse if I'd agreed with Nan, and
said there was something macabre about Aunt Lucy's bedroom.

"If you say so." Nan's hand dropped to her side.
"Lunch is ready. You'll feel better when you've had a bite
to eat."

Luncheon was a simple meal. Cold meat, biscuits and

cheese, with fresh fruit and a deep damson pie, clotted cream in a pottery bowl.

I found myself contemplating the portrait again, sure that the perfectly formed lips were smiling. Had they been smiling that morning? I tried to keep my voice as light as possible.

"Babs, have you noticed the portrait behind you? It's . . . unusual, isn't it?"

Babs was blissfully tucking into a generous helping of lamb. She spared a moment for the Georgian and then went back to her lunch.

"Is it? It seems ordinary enough to me."

"But he's very handsome. Almost excessively so, don't you think?"

Babs shrugged.

"He's good-looking, I suppose, but he's been dead a long time. No good to either of us."

"I didn't suggest he would be." I found myself as tart as quince. "I merely said the painting was unusual."

Babs stopped eating, eyeing me thoughtfully.

"Darling, you are jumpy. Why, you quite bit my head off then."

"Did I? I'm sorry." I forced myself to look away from the painted eyes. "I didn't mean to."

"First you hear moaning; then it's a smell. Now breathing, and . . ."

"How did you know that?" I snapped the words out. "Were you listening at my door, for I'm sure Nan wouldn't have told you?"

"I wasn't, but Dulcie was." Babs was quite shameless. "I swear you're getting as bad as your Aunt Lucy. Apparently she was very odd, poor old thing. I'm sorry about her, of course. Dulcie said she lay for a week in terrible pain, and her breathing could be heard all over the house. I really don't see how, since the walls are so thick, but that's what the girl said."

I put down a half-eaten biscuit, hiding my unsteady hands in my lap. An old woman dying in great pain, probably

moaning now and then, her breathing distressingly loud. It
didn't appear to have occurred to Babs that Lucy's end had
anything to do with what I had heard, but then how could
there be any connection?

I had never believed in ghosts, jeering at those who did,
but since I had arrived in Winterhill I was no longer so
sure.

" I wouldn't have liked to nurse her." Babs took more
meat, arranging it lovingly on her plate. " Dulcie told me
the smell was awful, as if she were rotting away."

I felt coldness run through my body like a streak of ice.
The moans, the breathing and now the smell. Could a house
retain the imprint of someone as faithfully as that? Was it
possible that the bedroom in which Aunt Lucinda had died
had kept the impression of her last days, waiting to turn it
loose on the next occupant?

I wished I hadn't been so stubborn earlier on. I should
have taken Nan's advice and changed rooms, but it was too
late now. I couldn't go back on what I'd said and admit how
frightened I was becoming. I tried to think of my father, to
stiffen my spine, but his face wouldn't come into my mind.
All I could see was a four-poster bed.

" By the way, Alex."

I was forced to pay attention to Babs, now spooning
cream on to a slice of pie.

" Yes?"

" It's tomorrow that we dine with Felix and his aunt."

" Is it?"

" You know it is! Do show some interest."

" I am."

"Well, what am I going to do?"

" Do?"

I stared at her vacantly, my thoughts slipping away, back
to the room on the first floor.

" Yes, about my dress. Do you think it will matter if I
wear the lilac again? Felix might not notice, but his aunt
will. So will the other women. They'll think me as poor as
a church mouse, which I am, of course."

I gave in without a struggle; it wasn't worth the effort of standing firm, despite what Nan had said.

"You can have my crimson, if you like."

"Crimson?" She wasn't satisfied: it wasn't what she wanted. "Do you think that would suit me? My hair is so fair, isn't it?" She patted it complacently. "Red might spoil it."

"Which one then?"

I wasn't even interested. I was looking at the Georgian again. He seemed to me to be more amused than ever, as if he were enjoying the spectacle of Babs twisting me round her little finger.

"That heavenly amber would be just right, but I know how awfully expensive it was. I don't suppose you'd want me to have that."

"Take it."

I didn't move as Babs got up, kissing me on the cheek, begging to be excused so that she could begin work on the gown. I just sat there, remembering what Babs had said earlier.

Aunt Lucy had died in pain; breathed so loudly that the maid had heard the sound beyond the four walls of the bedroom; had smelt as if she were rotting away.

"Oh my God," I covered my face with my hands, giving way to weakness for a moment. "What on earth is happening to me?"

*   *   *

It was a beautiful morning. The September sun was pure gold, and warm too, the sky as cloudless as if it were high summer.

Much to my surprise, I had slept well, and, if there had been sounds and smells, I hadn't been aware of them.

Babs was in high spirits. She had sat up late and finished her dress, remarking that it just needed the loan of my topaz pendant to make it perfect.

I nodded, hardly hearing her. I had made up my mind to

go to Farthing Wood again, no matter what Gavin had said of its reputation. I had no choice. I could let things crowd in on me, curling up like a terrified rabbit, or I could fight.

I took a shawl from the wardrobe, and went downstairs again and into the garden. When I reached the brook, I stopped to watch it for a while. So pure and clear, bubbling over the stones; untainted by the wood.

I crossed to the other bank and entered Farthing Wood. At first, nothing happened. For a time it seemed more like Cressy Wood had been. I bent and picked up leaves as I used to do, admiring the wonderful tints, crunching up the dried ones until they were powder in my hand. When I was young, I used to take a fistful home and pretend it was fairy dust, which could grant me any wish.

I reached a clearing and sat on a tree stump, glad that I hadn't given in. I was right to have come; everything was just as it should have been.

I don't know when the songs of the birds stopped, nor when the last squirrel vanished. It was only gradually that I realised there was total silence, and that the sun seemed to have gone in. The feeling of tension was back and all my efforts to be brave were gone too.

It was time to go. No matter how craven it was, I couldn't stay there a second longer.

I had only just started back when I heard the heart-beat. I knew it wasn't mine. Certainly, my own was pounding unbearably, but that wasn't what I was hearing. It was another's.

I looked behind me, aware before I did so that there wouldn't be anything to see. I was right. There were just trees, stretching back endlessly, and the feeling of dread increasing as the weird thudding hammered in my ears.

I promised myself I would not run. I walked quickly, trying not to panic, but it was no good. It seemed darker than ever and all my good intentions dissolved as I raced like a wild colt until I was clear of the wood.

Somehow I got back to the cottage, pausing for a moment until I was steadier. I did not want the others to know

what had happened. They already thought me hysterical;
even Nan, who had never doubted me before.

I recovered sufficiently to walk slowly upstairs to my room,
but a second later my hand was over my mouth, trying to
stop the spasm of terror.

I waited a second or two, unable to move: then I opened
the door again and called out.

When Nan, Babs and Kipps were all there, I said tightly:

"Which of you brought this up here? Who took it from
the dining-room?"

The others looked at the wall facing the bed, and the
portrait of the Georgian nobleman watching us all de-
risively.

Nan spoke first.

"Well I never! I swear it wasn't me, Miss Alex. Whyever
should I do a thing like that?"

"I don't know." I was fighting down a kind of primitive
fear. "But someone did. It didn't walk upstairs by itself.
Babs?"

"Don't be so silly." She was highly indignant. "Why
should I carry a heavy old thing like that up here? You must
have done it yourself. You seemed interested enough in the
wretched picture."

"Dulcie?"

"Not me, Miss."

The denial was quick and sounded genuine. I regarded
Dulcie uncertainly.

"Somebody must have done it," I said fretfully. "As I
say, it couldn't have got here by itself. Nan, are you sure ..."

"Of course I am." Nan was cross. "I'll not have you
blame me for this, Miss Alexandra. I'm not the one who
hears and sees things."

Nan only called me Alexandra when she was very put out,
and I sank down on the side of the bed, deflated.

"I'm sorry, I didn't mean to ... that is ..."

I couldn't stop the tears and Nan ordered Babs and Kipps
out of the room with a peremptory word.

"Now, now, my treasure." She held me close. "Don't you

take on so. Sorry if I was snappish just then, but I don't like this place any more than you do. No matter what you say, I know how you feel. Let's go to London, shall we?"

I dried my eyes, ashamed of myself. Children cried; fashionable young ladies of twenty-one did not.

"No, I won't be driven out. It must be my fancy, as you say. I'm staying here."

"And the picture?"

"I don't know how it got here, but let it be."

"I'll move it, if you want. Put it in the back extension, eh?"

The fate of the Georgian was in the balance. I looked up at his face; into the cool, satirical eyes. Then I shook my head.

"No, leave it where it is."

"If you say so. Well, if you're all right now, I've things to see to. You're dining out tonight, don't forget. I'd have a sleep after lunch if I were you. No sense in overdoing it."

As Nan closed the door, I heard the sigh once more. Faint, but triumphant, and I shivered from head to foot. Nan was right: we ought to go to London, but that would be to run away, as Ruth Segrave had run.

I paused, my fear temporarily forgotten. In such a small place as Winterhill, it was more than possible that Ruth had known Aunt Lucy. Visited her at the cottage; sat by her bed, perhaps reading to her. If that had been so, had Ruth heard and felt the things which I had done? If so, it was no wonder that the girl had gone. I made a mental note to ask Athene or Gavin if Ruth had called on my aunt, although I would never have the nerve to explain why I was enquiring.

Babs came into my room at eight, very pleased with herself in her new finery. She fingered the silver brushes and combs on the dressing-table, admiring the cut-glass powder-bowl and ring-holder.

"Aren't they lovely? I don't remember these."

"They were Aunt Lucy's."

"Yours now." Her voice had a rasp in it. "Like the cottage."

" Yes, I suppose so."

" I love cut-glass. When I marry a rich man, I shall have simply oceans of it everywhere. Do you think Felix is rich?"

" I've no idea. Babs, don't expect . . . well . . . that is . . . don't be too sure . . ."

" Of what?"

She turned abruptly, her flush a warning signal.

" Felix may not . . . that is . . . you can't be certain . . ."

" You always spoil things." She was livid with anger, recognising truth when she heard it. " Why shouldn't Felix like me, even love me? You're jealous."

" I'm not in the least jealous, and I'm sure that Mr Lancaster does like you. I don't want you to be hurt, that's all. He may not be contemplating marriage yet, or there may be someone else."

" I'm sure there isn't! You're hateful, Alex, quite hateful! You begrudge me the slightest happiness."

" You know I don't. Do be sensible. You've only just met him."

" Sensible?" The full mouth was smiling, but Babs was bent on hurting. " I'm sensible enough. Not like some who hear moaning and move pictures about the house."

" I didn't!"

" You said you did. You were shrieking out that night that you'd heard someone groaning and, when we got there, there wasn't a thing."

" I meant that I didn't move the picture. Do let's stop this; I don't want to quarrel with you."

" All right." Babs shook off her temper and gave a giggle, bargaining for the peace I desperately wanted. " I'll be good if you'll lend me your brocade bag for tonight: the gold one, I mean."

" Yes, take it. It's in the chest of drawers."

" So generous." The lips were curving upwards again. " Dearest Alex, so generous. And, after all, if you're right, and Felix doesn't want me, it won't matter all that much, will it? When you're dead, I shall have Lucy's Cottage, shan't I?"

FOUR

It was the night of my own dinner-party and Nan and Dulcie were helping me to dress.

At first, I'd had some doubts about the wisdom of trying to repay the hospitality of the Mortimers and Nadine Lancaster, wondering if Sheena Quinny were up to coping with a five-course meal. I need not have worried. Kipps told me, somewhat belatedly, that Sheena had been in the service of an earl's cousin, and I found that she was more than capable of preparing the dishes which I'd chosen.

I wished I could talk to Sheena; she must have been so lonely, but since she couldn't hear, talk or write I had to make do with a warm smile on the occasions when I saw her.

I had already inspected the table, laid with silver, crystal and porcelain. It would look quite splendid when the candles were lit.

I was almost relaxed as Nan helped me to put on the gown of ruby velvet, with the palest of blue faille underskirts. I wore pearls, lustrous and flattering the line of throat and breast, my hair drawn up to form a smooth knot at the back of my head.

Dulcie looked envious as she watched Nan twitch the train into position.

" Don't stand there gawping, girl." Nan seldom addressed Dulcie by name, for she had taken a thorough dislike to the maid, diminishing her importance to keep her in her place. " Get the shoes out of that wardrobe. At the bottom on the right: the crimson satin ones."

A minute later, Dulcie was screaming and I nearly jumped out of my skin, my fragile peace of mind totally shattered.

" Good heavens, what's the matter with you?" Nan got up quickly, astounded as Dulcie backed away from the wardrobe as if she had encountered a snake in its depths. "What on earth's wrong with you, you blockhead? You've given Miss Leith quite a turn."

But I was to grow more alarmed still when Dulcie mumbled fearfully about a garment which was lying screwed up on the floor of the vast cupboard.

" Nonsense!" Nan brushed the girl aside. "You're talking rubbish. How can you be so foolish? Here, let me see."

We all stared at the dress which Nan Ponsonby had pulled out and draped over her arm.

" That's the one I wore the day I came here." My voice wavered. "Nan, what's that dark stuff all over the bodice and sleeve?"

" It's blood." Nan's colour had gone too and her tone was not nearly as assured as it had been a minute or so before. " Dried blood, Miss Alex, that's what it is."

" It were hidden away." Dulcie was full of suspicion. " Pushed right down, as if it weren't meant to be seen."

" I don't understand." I was beginning to feel faint, but I knew I mustn't let Kipps see it. " How can it have got there?"

" How can what have got where?" Babs had come in, touching the amethysts she had borrowed once more, as if she were determined not to part with them. " Do you think I look nice? Oh! Nan, what's that? Alex, isn't that the new frock you wore when you arrived here?"

" Yes it is." I steeled myself to answer coolly. " It's got stains all over the top of it."

" Dried blood." Kipps's initial fear had gone and she was beginning to enjoy herself. She had seen through my efforts to disguise my dread and was going to make capital out of the situation. " Miss Ponsonby says it's blood."

Babs let out a shriek and was promptly silenced by Nan.

"That's enough, Miss Babs, quite enough. Girl, take this down to the scullery. I'll see to it later."

"But why has it got blood on it?" Babs waited until Dulcie had gone. "Did you cut yourself?"

"No."

"No, I would have noticed." Babs had seen my fear too, savouring it. "And, of course, a cut finger wouldn't make so large a stain. How on earth did you get it in that mess?"

"I didn't." My self-control was a crumbling thing, but grimly I held on to it. "When I took the frock off that day, there was nothing wrong with it. Since then, I've had no reason to look at it. I thought it was hanging up with the rest of my clothes."

"It was tucked down in one corner." Nan answered Babs's raised eyebrows. "The girl found it when she was getting Miss Alex's shoes. It's a rum do and no mistake."

"Alex!" Babs had started to smile, her pleasure growing. "What have you done?"

"I haven't done anything." I was rubbing my cheeks to get colour back into them. The guests would be arriving at any moment and I was in no fit state to receive them. "You know I haven't done anything."

"Well, we don't really, darling, do we?" She picked up a scent-bottle, eyes closed as she inhaled the expensive perfume. "What a gorgeous smell. You don't mind if I use some, do you?"

I watched her touch her ear-lobes and wrists, fighting down fresh alarm.

"What do you mean, you don't really know? You saw that there was nothing the matter with the dress when I got here."

Babs's lashes were lowered, concealing her expression.

"We didn't see the top of the frock. You wore a jacket over it, remember?"

"Yes, but . . ."

"And we have no idea what you were doing before you reached the cottage."

"Babs!" Anger was driving apprehension away. "You

know perfectly well what I was doing. I left the McAllisters at twelve o'clock and caught the train. Benson picked me up at Shottley and brought me here."

" Of course, but if, for instance, someone had been murdered, and the police were asking questions, could you prove it?"

" Certainly I could, and no one has been murdered." I needn't have bothered to try to bring a flush back to my cheeks; indignation was doing that for me. " Benson can verify that he met me at Shottley, and the McAllisters . . . oh!"

" Yes?"

Nan and Babs were watching me closely and I felt guilty; as if I were on trial.

" The McAllisters, Alex?"

" They left for India three days ago. Eventually, of course, they can confirm what I say, but not for a week or two. They've closed their house; sent the servants away."

" How exciting!" Babs was trying one of my tortoiseshell and diamond combs in her hair. " So, as they can't speak for you, you could have been anywhere that day, or even the night before. The only thing you can prove is that you were at Shottley Station when Benson arrived."

" Be quiet, Miss Babs!" Nan was furious. " What dreadful things to say! Put that comb down and get out of here. You're nothing but a spiteful little cat and, if I had my way, I'd send you home this very night."

" But you won't have your own way." Babs's own anger was cold and confident. She wasn't afraid of Nan, or me. " You're just a servant, and don't forget it."

Nan and I were silent for a whole, horrible minute after Babs had gone.

" It wasn't like that," I said finally. " I was with the McAllisters."

" Of course you were, and they'll say so when they can be reached. Now, put it out of your mind and come downstairs." She paused. " Still, it's a very funny thing, isn't it? Who'd take the trouble to come in here and hide that dress, and . . ."

" And how did the blood get on it? Yes, I know what you're thinking, but it wasn't me. Please go down; I want to be by myself for a moment."

She was reluctant to leave, but in the end she did, and I sat down and looked at myself in the mirror. It occurred to me that since I'd arrived at Lucy's Cottage I'd spent a good deal of time gazing in the looking-glass, and it had nothing to do with conceit. It was almost as though I wanted re-assurance that I was same person I'd always been.

I doubted if Babs had been responsible for ruining the dress; she wouldn't have spoilt a perfectly good outfit which one day she might have been able to acquire for herself. Dulcie had turned green at the first sight of blood, and Sheena was a pathetic creature, with no malice in her.

Someone must have got into the house, even if there had been no sign of forced entry. There was no other explanation. As I applied more rouge, I could see the tremor in my fingers. The villagers wouldn't come to Lucy's Cottage, never mind force an entry. They were too afraid of it.

I got up, knowing I had to pull myself together and be ready with a warm welcome for my guests, but I hadn't time to turn away from the dressing-table when it happened.

" So beautiful. My love, you are so very beautiful."

I watched my lips part, my eyes dilate: transfixed, and unable to move.

That same odd whisper, not like a real voice, but loud enough to hear. A gentle murmur from behind me, in an empty room. I was rigid, my throat closing. There wasn't a soul there; I was still alone.

I don't know why I looked up at the Georgian; it was quite instinctive. In the soft light of the lamps, the mouth was humorous, almost tender. Despite my paralysis, I found myself wondering what he had been like to kiss, knowing beyond doubt that he would have been an exciting lover.

Finally I was able to pick up my fan. I had to get out of the room without delay. I would ask Nan and Kipps to transfer my things to a spare room; I wouldn't spend another night here. But it was no good. It was as if some outside force were filling my mind, my decision melting away, leaving me helpless. I wouldn't be able to change rooms. I should have to stay, for this was where I belonged.

On the way downstairs, my mind was in a turmoil. Was it real, that soft voice, or was it only in my head? Whatever else was my imagination, the bloodstains on my dress were genuine enough, and I had no idea how they had got there. Could anyone get such stains all over themselves and not remember a thing about it?

As the first knock on the door came, I hurried to the drawing-room. I had to put everything behind me for a few hours and not let anyone guess what I was feeling.

But, even as I heard the sound of voices outside, my lips were forming a word. A single name, and my heart nearly stopped.

" Ruth."

I don't know whether I spoke aloud, or to myself, but inside I was praying frantically. "Dear God, don't let the blood be Ruth's. Oh, please, please, don't let it be Ruth's!"

*   *   *

The sight of my guests, and the laughter and chatter, seemed to lift the burden from me at once. The lower rooms had none of the atmosphere of Lucy's bedroom and I could be normal again. It was like stepping from one world into the next and I was very glad to see Gavin.

" I wish you'd invited me alone." He kissed my hand, holding it too long. " I want you to myself."

" But think of my reputation." I was even able to flirt discreetly, despite the experience I had just had; Gavin made it easy. " We are alone when we ride."

" So we are. Shall we take the horses up to Portsleigh Hill tomorrow?"

" Not tomorrow. I . . . I may be tired after tonight."

His eyes narrowed faintly.

" You're not ill?"

" No, of course not."

" Nor upset? You seem . . . oh damn! Here's Nadine and my mother. We'll talk later."

The dinner was a great success.

" I'd no idea Sheena had it in her." Nadine was sipping her wine, clearly amazed to find that Lucinda's cellar could produce such an excellent claret. " I suppose your aunt didn't entertain, so the poor woman never had the chance to cook anything but rice pudding."

" No, I suppose not. She has done well though."

" Best meal I've had for a long time." Max gave me a friendly grin. " Glad you've settled in so well, m'dear. Always nice to have a new face in the village, especially a pretty one like yours, eh, Athene?"

" Yes, indeed." Athene was in strident green, with outrageous beads and silver earrings several inches long. She should have looked a fright, but she didn't. The grace of her movements, and the strong personality she exuded, rose above her refusal to bow to fashion.

" I'd like to paint you one day. You've been told I dabble, I expect."

" Yes." I was struck yet again by her deep voice, fascinated by the eyes like slivers of precious gems which held mine. " Gavin says you're most talented."

" He exaggerates, of course, but will you sit for me?"

" I don't think I'd make a very good subject. Perhaps Miss Wycombe?"

Athene glanced at Babs. It wasn't necessary for her to speak; it was all too obvious what she thought about my companion.

Babs bridled and at once Felix Lancaster sprang to her defence.

" If I could paint, I'd ask Miss Wycombe to sit for me." He gave Athene a black look. " I think she'd make a most excellent study."

Nadine made short work of his gallantry.

" But then you know nothing about art, do you, my dear? Yes, I will have the tiniest bit more of the compote of peaches, if I may. It's quite delicious, and I hope you'll let Sheena give me the recipe. No, Felix, I think you should concentrate on your studies. If you are ever to become a lawyer, you'll have no time for portrait-painting, or any other trivial affairs."

I saw Babs's fury and stepped in quickly.

"Tell me, Colonel, is there any more news of Ruth Segrave? Has she been found?"

I asked, not only to save Babs further embarrassment, but because I desperately wanted to know. If Ruth was safe, I could stop worrying about the stained dress.

"Not yet, I'm afraid."

My heart sank.

"And her brother?"

"No word from him either. It's obvious he didn't get the telegram. Poor child; I hope she's all right, wherever she is."

"Don't you think that the police should be told now? Time is passing."

I felt as though I was digging my own grave; then I checked myself. Whoever put the stains on the gown, it wasn't me, and I would write to the McAllisters that very night, sending the letter to Delhi to await their arrival.

My question brought the same silence that it had done before, but I wasn't deterred.

"It is the wisest course, surely, if she isn't with relatives."

"There are only two cousins and an old aunt; they haven't had time to reply yet. As to the police, well, I doubt if you'd suggest going to them if you knew Richard Segrave. A hard man; hard as nails. Keeps himself aloof from us, up there in that great house of his. Doesn't want to mix. Family's very old, of course; old and proud. If we informed the police without his knowledge, I wouldn't like to answer for what would happen. Don't you agree, Geoffrey?"

Thatcher had said nothing so far. Self-effacing as ever, he seemed to merge into the background, as if he didn't want to be seen, but now he raised his head.

"Yes, you're right. Segrave wouldn't thank us for interfering. Better leave things as they are until he gets home."

" Yes, yes." Nadine was swift to confirm. " Of course, Miss Leith couldn't be expected to realise what Sir Richard is like. Naturally, in other circumstances, one would have informed the authorities, although, as I've said before, the child may have gone off to one of the cousins without bothering to tell anyone. She was a funny little thing, and we mustn't jump to conclusions."

" Quite right." George Carlton was mopping his brow, as if he were uncomfortably warm. " May be some perfectly ordinary reason why she went, and the servants at The Hall aren't doing anything, except trying to trace Segrave. We ought not to meddle."

" I expect Sir Richard will be back soon anyway; he and his friends." Max was reassuring me, anxious not to let me feel I'd been snubbed. " Don't you worry; he'll be home before long to see to things."

" Do tell us, Miss Leith," said Gillian, turning another awkward pause away. " Have you seen anything since you came here?" She gave a nervous laugh. " Do you know, when your kind invitation came, I almost didn't accept, for one has heard such strange things about this house. Then I thought that I'd be with so many friends, I could chance it. Well, have you seen anything?"

The others were waiting and I could feel all eyes on me. I had to be careful. It was no good lying outright, because Kipps would have told the tradesmen about my moans and smells and the heart-beat, and such news would have travelled quickly. By tomorrow, the whole village would know about the blood-stained dress, but that could wait for another day.

" I did think I'd heard a noise," I said warily, " but my maid assures me it was only the ivy outside my window, or perhaps a draught in the chimney."

" How awful for you!" Clearly, Gillian was torn between sympathy and the delightful prospect of another snippet of information about the house which she could mull over with her cronies. " I should have left at once, I'm sure."

" I shall get used to it. After all, Aunt Lucinda lived here for years, quite happily. Colonel Mortimer has told me that the reason why she didn't go out was because she was old and tired. She wasn't afraid of the cottage."

Carlton cleared his throat, still ill at ease.

" Hm. Yes, he was right, at least, almost right."

"George!" Nadine pounced on him at once, trying to undo the damage. "We don't want to go into all that."

"All what?" I was alert and on edge, sensing trouble. " What do you mean, Dr Carlton?"

"Nadine, it's no good hiding it from the gel. She's got to live here and, if we don't tell her, others will. I'm surprised that that maid, what's-her-name, hasn't done so already. Or maybe she has?"

I wouldn't let myself cringe. I was in a roomful of people, and Gavin, sitting next to me, was holding my hand under the damask cloth. Nothing could hurt me.

" Tell me what?"

"No, George, I think Nadine's right." The colonel was brusque. " Let it rest. Lucinda's dead now, and there's no point in raking it all up again."

"All what?" I knew I was growing shrill, in spite of my determination to remain composed. "Please, Colonel Mortimer, if Dr Carlton has something to tell me about my aunt, let him do so. I have a right to know. What happened to her?"

" Happened to her?" Carlton scowled. " I didn't say anything happened to her."

"Then what did you mean? Please do explain properly what you are talking about."

Athene sighed.

"Gillian, I do wish you'd think before you speak. If you hadn't asked that idiotic question, none of this need have been mentioned." She ignored Gillian's stricken face. "You'd better tell her now, George; the harm's done."

"Yes?" I was still gripping Gavin's hand. "What about my aunt, Dr Carlton?"

Carlton scratched his beard, clearly reluctant to go on.

" She was a good woman, no one could say otherwise, but in the last two years of her life she grew odd. No, more than that; almost fey. She said she couldn't leave her bedroom. Claimed she had heard queer things in Farthing Wood too; that's why she stopped going there."

"You said she didn't dislike the wood." I turned to Max indignantly. "You said it was because her bones ached that she didn't go out. Dulcie was right after all."

"I know, I know." Mortimer gave Mrs Baxter an exasperated look. "I didn't want you to worry. After all, you're only here for a few months, aren't you, and we all hoped that it wouldn't be necessary for you to know."

I sank back and let Gavin's hand go. His support was useless now.

"You hoped I wouldn't find out that my aunt was mad, is that what you're saying?"

"Not mad," said Max quickly, "just . . ."

"She was quite mad." Nadine was very firm. "Max, for heaven's sake be honest with Miss Leith." She looked at me almost sympathetically. "It's a pity you had to find out. As Max says, we all hoped to spare you. Lucinda Oakley was quite off her head. How Kipps and Quinny ever managed to look after her, I'll never know. And the things she did! Why, once she managed to drag a heavy old painting out of the dining-room and up to her room. I can't imagine how, or why, but she must have been a good deal stronger than she looked. And another time, they found a shawl of hers in a drawer, covered in dried blood. What she'd been up to, no one ever found out."

The room was swaying dangerously and I felt very sick. Gavin said tersely:

"For God's sake, Nadine, that's enough. Can't you see what you're doing?"

I was helped to an armchair and made to drink brandy. Gradually, the faintness passed and the room came into focus again.

"I'm so sorry." I'd never heard Nadine use such a soft voice, contrite as she patted my hand. "I should have been more careful what I was saying. Do forgive me."

"Of course." I had to forget what she'd said, or I would

c

have begun to shake again. " Don't think another word about
it. I wanted to know. Since you've been so frank, please tell
me if there is anything else. I'd rather know now, and get
it over."

Nadine nodded approvingly.

" You're a sensible gel and you are right. Best to know it
all, and then put it behind you."

Athene said slowly :

" There's not much more to tell, really. Her mind had
gone, poor old thing, and it was only because the two maids
looked after her so well that she wasn't put away. Oh yes,
there was one other thing. She said something very strange
to Dr Carlton, just before she died. George?"

He didn't want to answer, but I had to know.

" Please, Dr Carlton, I'm quite all right now and I do
want to hear. What did Aunt Lucy say to you?"

" Don't know that it's wise to . . ."

" Please!"

He gave up, obviously hating every minute of the conversation.

" Very well. She said she wouldn't leave this cottage when
she was dead. That whoever came after her would find her
still here. Said they'd feel her, and hear her, and she'd never
go." He put his glasses on, trying not to look at me. " She
didn't know what she was saying, I can assure you, for she
was delirious. A sick old woman, Miss Leith; it meant
nothing."

" Of course it didn't." Athene was urging me to drink hot
black coffee. " Come, dear, don't leave any; it'll do you
good."

" I'm so sorry to have made such a fool of myself." I could
hardly hold the cup, for my hands felt frozen and every last
thing which I had been told about Aunt Lucy was burning
into my brain like drops of acid. " I've quite spoilt the
party."

They all denied it loudly, trying to turn the conversation
to other things, but Babs wouldn't let them.

" Now, isn't that extraordinary?" she said, eyes round as

saucers, and very innocent. "The other day, a picture which
was in the dining-room was found hanging on the wall of
Alex's bedroom. We still don't know who took it upstairs,
but Alex had been admiring it so much that I thought it
must be her."

I wanted to shout at Babs to be quiet, but the damage was
done. Almost imperceptibly, the others were drawing back.
A little at first, then further away, but Babs hadn't finished.

"I'll tell you another remarkable thing." She smiled at
me, and I could read the hate in her. "Alex's mother showed
me a portrait of Miss Oakley which had been done when she
was about Alex's age."

"I see nothing odd about that." Gavin was the only one
who hadn't moved away. He had taken Athene's place by my
side, holding my hand regardless of who was watching.
"Many people have their portraits painted."

"Of course." Babs was full of sugary apology. "I didn't
mean to throw any doubts on Alex, but it was so peculiar.
You see, Lucinda Oakley was the mirror-image of Alex. If
you'd seen the painting, you'd have agreed. One simply
couldn't tell them apart."

*   *   *

I lay staring into the darkness. It was beginning to make
an awful kind of sense, that is, if one believed in the super-
natural.

There were too many things happening for them to be
real coincidences; it had to be more than that.

Aunt Lucy had been peculiar. No, that was an understate-
ment; she had been demented. As she lay dying, she had
told her doctor that she wouldn't leave the cottage. It was
just what I had wondered after the moans, the heart-beat
and the smell. Could the room still contain traces of Lucinda?
Did the walls, the floor, the ceiling, retain a part of my
great-aunt, hiding her away where she couldn't be seen?

No one else heard, felt or sensed anything, only me. So
Lucy had stayed for me, and for none other.

I sat up abruptly, sleep very far off, lighting a candle and reaching for the book on the bedside table.

I hadn't even had time to open the volume before I felt the chill in the room. It was just as if a window had been opened, letting in the cold night ·air. I drew back as the curtains billowed out, certain that there must be someone behind them. I was wrong. After a second or two, they fell slackly into place again.

"Don't be afraid." As soft as ever and just as clear. " I'm here, and I won't let anything hurt you."

It was a long time before I could get out of bed. I knew better than to call Nan or Babs, for there would be no sound in the room, once they had arrived. The whisper, with such an eerie quality, was for me, not for them.

I pulled the curtains back, finding nothing but darkness beyond the windows; then I looked at the bed where Lucy had died in agony.

Everything was just as it had been on the day my great-aunt had gone to her Maker; Dulcie had told me that. Nothing had been changed. Nothing, that is, except the portrait on the wall, which, presumably, had been returned to the dining-room after Kipps had found it in her mistress's room. Odd that Dulcie hadn't told me of the incident when I demanded to know who had brought the Georgian upstairs. Perhaps the girl had been too frightened by the repetition of what had happened once before, to speak.

A shawl with blood on it. I was so unsteady that I got back into bed in case my legs gave way. Whose blood had been on Lucy's shawl, and whose on my dress?

I looked up at the picture, wishing that he were of flesh and blood so that I could talk to him, for I desperately needed the comfort of another human being. But he had died a long time ago. As Babs had said; he was no good to either of us.

After what seemed an eternity, I began to feel very tired, lids heavy and closing against my will. At least Lucy didn't seem to dislike me. She had said that I was beautiful, and, if it had been she who had spoken when I had run out of the wood, she had also promised twice to protect me.

Sleep came at last, washing over me and carrying me away in merciful arms. I was grateful; so grateful that, when the whisper came again, I didn't stir.

Yet the next morning, when I was dressing, I remembered the words as if they had just been spoken.

"Good night, my love, good night. I'll watch until the morning."

Lucy had kept her promise. She hadn't left the cottage.

FIVE

The following night I dreamt again. It was worse this time, for I wasn't in Lucy's bedroom, but in a dark, confined space.

There were others there, but I didn't know how many, or who they were. Their faces were shadowed, so that I couldn't see them clearly; all I was aware of were eyes, staring at me.

I could feel myself being lifted up, helpless and unable to resist; a door was closing and I was alone in what seemed to be a tomb.

I almost cried with relief when I woke up. The nightmare had been so real that I had been certain I'd been left to die. When I had stopped shaking, I sat up and poured myself a glass of water, determined not to fall asleep again that night.

In those flat, hateful hours before dawn, I tried to think rationally about what had happened to me since I had arrived at Winterhill, but it was not easy to be sensible.

The real fear lay in Lucinda Oakley's bedroom and in Farthing Wood. In the rest of the house, in the village and in other people's homes things were normal enough. I knew quite well that I should have moved to a spare room, but, immediately I made the decision to do so, something seemed to stop me. My own will, which I had always thought a strong one, was pitted against a force stronger still.

I considered the possibility of the whole business being created by a human agency. If Babs disliked me as much as Gavin said she did, and I was bound to agree that he was right, she could have brought the painting up to my room. She could have slipped in and out of the bedroom without me actually seeing her: it was not wholly beyond the bounds of possibility that she had been responsible for the sounds and smells, although how she had achieved it I had no idea. She could certainly have put animal's blood on my dress.

But Babs couldn't get into my mind and manufacture bad dreams; no one could do that. For a second I went cold at the thought of that enclosed space in which I'd been locked. Was I looking back at the past, or seeing into the future?

In the end, I rejected Babs. If she had spoken to me, it wouldn't have been in a kindly way, and she certainly wouldn't have told me that I was beautiful.

But at breakfast-time the doubts came back. Babs was watching me closely, even neglecting her food. It seemed to me in my unhappiness that she was waiting for me to show some sign of breaking under the stress, and that when she asked me if I'd slept well her question was malicious.

" Very well, thank you." I had no intention of letting her see my worry. " And it's such a lovely morning that I think I'll go for a walk."

" Not again!" Babs went back to her eggs and bacon. " You'll overtire yourself, and then you'll start hearing things once more."

I ignored her and left the house by the back door. I looked down at Farthing Wood, but I couldn't face it that day. Instead, I went up the hill towards Possett's Farm, watching a girl in a gingham frock feeding pigs. Her apron was grubby, her hair blowing in her eyes, but she looked rosy and contented, and I envied her.

When I got back, Nan was waiting for me in the hall.

" You've got a visitor."

She sounded nervous and instantly I was on my guard again. It wasn't like Nan.

" Oh? Who is it? Mr Mortimer?"

" No, it's Sir Richard Segrave. You know, the one whose sister's missing. He's back, and he wants to see you."

I hesitated at the door of the sitting-room, reluctant to meet Ruth's brother. I didn't know why, unless it was because I'd been warned about his somewhat unfriendly disposition. Perhaps it was because of my disturbed rest that

I felt dismay at confronting him. Confronting him? Even the word which sprang to my mind was odd. Why should I think of our meeting in those terms?

"Sir Richard?"

He was standing by the window, looking out, but turned at once, coming to the centre of the room.

It seemed a very long time before he spoke. I was staring at him, not just because he was so different from what I had pictured, but because I felt an instant attraction, so strong and compelling that I knew my life had changed in that single second.

He was tall and elegant. Not startlingly handsome, like my Georgian, but good to look at, with hair the colour of dark honey, and hazel eyes with no warmth in them. It was a thin, clever face, with a firm chin, and lines at the corners of his mouth which made it look bitter. I could understand the others' judgment now; it wouldn't be easy to get close to this man.

"Yes. Miss Leith?"

He was crisp and businesslike, wasting no time on preliminaries, not even welcoming me to Winterhill as we sat down.

"You know that my sister is missing?"

"Yes." I sat up very straight in my own chair, not relaxing a muscle in case he should trap me somehow. "Yes, I know, and I'm very sorry. I'm told that she ran away."

"So I hear." He hadn't taken his eyes off me once, and I was growing more uncomfortable still. "I have only just got back, but my neighbours haven't been slow in giving me their theories."

"But you don't think she did run away?"

"I don't know yet. That's what I'm trying to find out."

"Why have you come to me? I didn't know your sister. She'd gone before I arrived."

"Do you know Simeon New?"

His tone warned me that he wasn't lightly to be turned aside.

"No, who is he?"

" An old man who has lived here all his life; knows everyone and everything about the village. He says he saw Ruth running towards this house. Saw her go in, but although he waited for a long time she didn't come out again."

" But that's impossible!" I rejected New's story at once. " When was this?"

" The day she disappeared."

" How could the man be so sure? It was dark; he could have been mistaken in thinking it was your sister."

His lids dropped slightly and I felt a prick of nervousness. My pulse was racing in a way that it had never done before. He was frightening me, but he was having another, and quite extraordinary, effect on me too.

I had never believed in love at first sight, for it seemed to me to be an absurd conception. The initial meeting with another human being couldn't fill the mind with such sensuous thoughts, nor make the heart quicken until it flooded one's whole being with joy. I had declared such a situation to be pure nonsense, but now I knew that I'd been wrong.

I looked away quickly, in case he could read in me the first, breathtaking realisation of passion. I didn't want this unfriendly stranger to realise what he'd done to me; to know that I should never be the same person again because some mysterious chemistry between us had altered my whole being. It wasn't only because he was comely : I'd met many handsome men. I didn't understand what it was. I was simply conscious of a fierce desire of a kind no respectable young female should know existed.

" How did you know it was dark, Miss Leith?" His voice was very soft, cutting through my bewilderment. " I didn't say so."

I was instantly confused, both by the snare he had laid and because he was close to me.

" I just assumed it was."

" I see. Well, your assumption was correct."

He seemed in no hurry to go on, as if he knew how

vulnerable I was. I didn't know where to look, and the second lesson I learned about love was painful. It wasn't all happiness, as I had supposed. This man, who had turned my world upside down, didn't share what I was feeling. He was totally indifferent to me and probably always would be.

"Nadine Lancaster tells me that Ruth often visited your aunt. Did you know that? I must confess that I was unaware of it."

I was glad the silence had been broken, trying to regain my self-possession. I had wondered if Ruth had been in Lucy's bedroom: now I knew.

"No, she didn't mention it to me."

"It seems she did. She became very friendly with Miss Oakley. Nadine says Ruth told her that your aunt had grown so fond of her, that she was going to leave this cottage to her. Miss Oakley said she'd made a second will, properly witnessed, and had hidden it in this house for safety."

It was like a blow in the pit of my stomach and I didn't know what to say. I felt like an intruder in another woman's house; an unwanted invader. Lucy hadn't meant me to have her cottage at all; she'd left it to Ruth Segrave. Finally, I got a grip on myself.

"I don't understand. Where is the second will? Why did my aunt's solicitors write and tell me that I'd inherited the cottage?"

"For the simple reason that the second will was never found, according to Miss Lancaster. A thorough search was undertaken, but there was no trace of it. No one knows who the witnesses were either, it seems. Therefore, the first will was the only valid document."

"I don't know what to say. I had no idea."

"Hadn't you?" He was clipped; disbelieving. "Ruth also told Nadine that your aunt had written to tell you what she intended to do; some three months before she died."

"I received no such letter."

"What letter, Alex? Oh, do forgive me; I suppose I shouldn't have interrupted you."

I gave a start. I'd been so absorbed in Segrave, and what

he'd been saying, that I hadn't noticed Babs had come in.
Segrave rose, acknowledging her with a slight bow.

She dimpled at him, looking fresh and pretty in spotted
foulard, wearing my perfume which scented the air as she
took a seat next to me.

I couldn't remember being so angry with her as I was at
that moment. I wanted Richard to myself, no matter how
abrupt he was. It was an effort to introduce them, but I
managed it somehow.

I could tell Segrave was annoyed at the interruption too,
but for different reasons.

" I was sorry to hear about your sister." Babs had a thick
skin and she had no intention of leaving. " I do so hope
she'll return soon. What letter, Alex?"

I almost told her to mind her own business. She was
everywhere, poking her nose into things which didn't concern her; pawing my belongings; stabbing at me with that
sharp tongue of hers. I could have asked her to leave us,
but that would have meant a week of sulks and perhaps
worse. It was difficult, too, not to explain what Lucy had
done, for I knew I'd get no peace until she'd wormed it out
of me.

" But I didn't get the letter and so I knew nothing about
it," I concluded, wishing again that I didn't feel an out-
sider in my own home. " It's all most unfortunate."

" How long ago did Miss Oakley write to you?"

Babs was admiring Sir Richard with a predatory air and
for the first time in my life I knew what jealousy felt like.
It was a dreadful, tearing emotion, destructive to mind and
soul. I was willing Babs to go away and leave Richard alone.
Even if he were suspicious of me, I wanted all his attention.
I didn't want to share any part of him with Babs.

" About three months before she died, Sir Richard says.
Miss Lancaster told him."

Babs began to count on her fingers and I knew by her
expression that she was about to make trouble.

" Why, that would be about Christmas time." Her gaze
was limpid. " I was staying with you at the villa then, don't

you remember? I can recall quite clearly that one morning, just before you came down to breakfast, your mother was looking through the post. She said that there was a letter for you, and then she said: ' It's from Aunt Lucinda—Lucy, we call her. I wonder what she wants.' "

I wished I could sink through the floor, but escape was not that easy.

" I didn't get such a letter." I repeated it as firmly as I could. " My mother didn't mention it to me."

" Isn't that peculiar?" Babs was artless, talking to no one in particular. " Whyever should she hold back your letters?"

" I'm sure she didn't."

" Then you must have had it." Babs was purring as she set out to make the situation worse. " But perhaps your mind was getting a bit confused even then."

Segrave's icy glance moved to Babs, and he was demanding an explanation from her, using no words.

She responded willingly.

" Well, you see . . ."

" Babs! Please!"

" I'm sorry, dear, I didn't think you wanted it kept a secret."

It made things sound more sinister still, and I was forced into some kind of explanation.

" It's nothing, Sir Richard, and certainly has no connection with the letter which you say my aunt wrote to me. I just thought I'd heard noises in the bedroom I'm occupying, but I'm sure I must have been mistaken."

Segrave was studying me again, no vestige of expression on his face. I would have given anything to know what he was thinking, but there was no hope of that. He was the kind of person who kept his own countenance.

" You arrived the day my sister disappeared, didn't you?"

" No." Babs hadn't finished yet. " No, Alex came the next afternoon. She'd been staying with friends, so she told Nan, her maid, and me."

" I was visiting friends." I was stony. " Babs, I think I would like you to go now."

"All right, darling, if you say so. But you could have been here in Winterhill the night before, couldn't you?"

The attack was so vicious that I was stunned. Babs was no longer being petty, or hinting at things in private. Now she was setting out to injure me publicly.

"It's possible," I said finally, when I could trust myself to speak, "but I wasn't. Please go."

"Oh very well. Good-bye, Sir Richard. I do hope we shall meet again. I'm sure we shall, and I shall look forward to it."

I felt hot anger flood through me again as Segrave rose, waiting until she had gone.

"Yes, you could have been here the night before, couldn't you?"

"I wasn't, I can assure you. My friends can verify that, when . . ."

He was quick to pick me up.

"When? When what?"

"When I can reach them. They've gone to India, but they only left a day or two ago. I don't know which route they're taking, or whether they intend to stop anywhere."

"How convenient!"

His disbelief was like a wound. I was crying inside at the unfairness of life. My experiences since I had come to Winterhill had been bad enough; now I had met a man whose mere existence had changed the pattern of my being, and he was looking at me as if I had been responsible for removing his sister. Looking at me as if he hated me.

I had to feign anger or I should have burst into tears.

"Sir Richard, why should I lie? I know nothing about your sister. Why do you assume that I had anything to do with what has happened?"

"If you knew that your aunt intended to leave the cottage to Ruth, and if you knew the second will was hidden here, and no doubt your aunt's letter said as much, then you had a reason to wish Ruth out of the way."

"This is preposterous!" My anger was genuine that time. "I'd never heard of your sister, as I've just told you. If I'd thought the second will might be found, I would have come to England before this, wouldn't I?"

"There was no need. The solicitors had told you that you'd inherited it, yet, on reflection, you may have been afraid that Ruth would keep looking."

"This is incredible." I stood up, wanting to shake him to make him believe me. "I didn't want the cottage that much. Who would?"

After a second or two, he said quietly:

"Ruth did, apparently. I'm told she was obsessed by it. I hadn't realised it myself, but Miss Lancaster has informed me that my sister thought about little else. She told Nadine that she lived for the day when it would be hers."

My fury died as quickly as it had come. Richard had sadness and worry in him beneath the surface, and I wanted to console him, but of course I couldn't. I forced my thoughts away from him for a second. Another who wanted Lucy's Cottage with a violent and frightening intensity, just like Babs.

"I see. I didn't realise that, naturally, but it makes no difference. Even if I did come to make another search, somewhat late in the day, what if I'd found it? It would simply mean that Ruth would have got her wish."

"Would it?"

He was bleak again, giving me no quarter, and the lump in my throat was larger.

"Of course. Do you suppose that I would try to hold on to a property which wasn't mine?"

"I don't know. It would depend how much you wanted it for yourself."

"Not very much. I thought when I first came here that I would love it; now I'm not so sure."

"This place has a reputation, you know; even I'm aware of that. It's said that those who possess it never let it go."

I sank down in my chair, feeling thoroughly wretched and miserable because I couldn't make the slightest dent in his armour.

"I don't want Lucy's Cottage in that way. I don't know

whether you believe me, and I don't much care." It was
wholly untrue, because I cared terribly what he thought.
" It's the truth. It's also the case that I never saw your sister;
never did her any harm. If I'd known Aunt Lucy had wanted
her to have the house, I would never have come to England
at all. Now, if you have nothing else to say. . . ."

I was urging him silently to go, before the tears started.

" Not at the moment, but I may want to talk to you
again."

" And I may be prepared to receive you."

As he opened the door, our hands touched, for I too was
reaching for the knob, wanting him to hurry before I dis-
graced myself.

It was like a fierce current running through me and I drew
back as if I'd been burnt.

" I beg your pardon." He was frigid, quite misunder-
standing the gesture. " Good day, Miss Leith."

* * *

" Babs, you were quite intolerable, just now."

I was getting ready for lunch, Babs sitting at the dressing-
table trying on my pearls.

" Oh, surely not." Her head was on one side, admiring
herself. " I only said . . ."

" I'm well aware of what you said. You made me sound
like a criminal or a half-wit. I'm sure Sir Richard thinks I
had a hand in his sister's disappearance, and it's all your
fault."

She wasn't in the least peeved; far from it.

" Well, it is a bit odd, isn't it? And if he'd known about
the blood on the frock you wore the day you arrived he'd be
even more doubtful, wouldn't he?"

" I'm surprised you didn't tell him about that too," I
returned bitterly, " you kept precious little else to yourself.
You seem to be going out of your way to create doubts about
me, and I won't have it. If it doesn't stop, I shall send you
away."

" You can't." She laid the pearls down with a regretful sigh. " Your mother wouldn't let you do that. I should have to send her a wire, if you tried to get rid of me. Besides, it's even more important that I stay with you now, because of. . . ."

" Because of what?"

I could have boxed her ears.

" Well, you're not yourself, are you. Hearing and smelling things which aren't there. You need me."

Then she did look up, and I was shaken. She was as cold and unyielding as iron.

" Even Nan thinks you want looking after. May I wear these tonight?"

" No."

" If I could, I might forget to tell Sir Richard about that dress of yours. Why, Alex, you look quite wan. Don't you think Sir Richard is a fascinating man? I could so easily fall in love with someone like him. Perhaps I will."

The blind fury I felt at her words shook me. Babs even talking of such a thing made me want to claw her smooth, plump cheeks and draw blood. For a second, I wondered if she had read in me my unexpected reaction to Segrave, but that wasn't possible. She was just drooling over another good-looking man; wanting him. But I wanted him too.

Suddenly I stiffened, Richard forgotten. The smell was back; horrible, permeating, like a grave. I gave Babs a quick glance, expecting to find her wrinkling her nose in disgust, but she hadn't been aware of the whiff of death, if that was what it was. Only I could smell it; it was meant for me.

" We'd better go down," I said finally. " Lunch will be ready."

" Good, I'm hungry. May I borrow the necklace?"

Our eyes met and we both knew it was a battle. I ought to have resisted, but I didn't want Richard to be more doubtful of me than he was already.

" Very well."

" Poor Alex." Babs was triumphant, well aware of her

success. " How tired you look! Maybe Nan was right. You
ought to see a doctor before it's too late."

* * *

Gavin, and Gillian Baxter, called at tea-time. Gavin's
warmth helped to dispel the depression which had beset me,
but Gillian was full of concern at my appearance.

" So washed-out, dear," she said anxiously. " I hope you're
eating properly. You young things don't look after yourselves; always afraid of spoiling your figures."

" Yes, I'm eating." I lied as I poured the tea. " I didn't
sleep very well last night, that's all."

" Alex has bad dreams." Babs helped herself to the hot,
buttered scones which Dulcie was offering her. " I've heard
her cry out."

" Do you?" Gavin frowned. " What sort of dreams?"

I had no choice but to continue to be untruthful.

" I've no idea; I didn't know I had dreamt. Mrs Baxter,
do have another, please."

" Yes, I think I will, although my dressmaker was scold-
ing me only last week because I'd put a whole inch on round
the waist."

That made me think of Lucia, and suddenly I wanted to
be back in Florence with her, telling her all about Lucinda's
bedroom and my nightmares. Lucia looked ethereal, fragile
and totally helpless, but she was self-sufficient, well-organised
and possessed of the soundest common sense I'd ever known.
I made up my mind there and then to write to her; her
answer would soon put my fancies to flight.

" I hear Sir Richard came to see you to-day." Gillian
was agog and I suspected that we were now getting to the
real reason for her visit. " What did you think of him? Such
a cold man, I always think. I can't understand him leaving
that poor child with a companion and a housekeeper, whilst
he went gallivanting across Europe with those friends of his.
He couldn't have cared a button for her."

" Couldn't? You talk as if she were dead."

Mrs Baxter was shocked.

" Miss Leith, I didn't mean any such thing, although I do wonder, seeing it's been so long. No, no, I expect she'll come back soon." She was caught off balance at being picked up so quickly. " I just meant that her brother was very off-hand."

" I thought he seemed quite concerned." I was amazed that I could sound so indifferent when speaking of Richard. His very name filled me with a glow I'd never known before. I wanted to shout to the meddlesome Mrs Baxter that I loved him and didn't want to hear criticisms of him. That would have silenced her effectively, but, of course, I did no such thing. " He is most anxious to find her."

" I think he believes Alex knows about her disappearance." Babs's air of genuine concern would have put many a professional actress to shame. " He said that she might have been here in Winterhill the night Ruth went."

" But that's impossible." Gavin was curt. " Alex didn't arrive until the following afternoon. The man must be mad."

" No, he's far from that." I couldn't let even Gavin say such things, and explained how Simeon New had seen Ruth running towards the cottage, trying to defend Segrave. " I don't think he meant to accuse me; he's just worried."

Gavin was still angry, but Gillian got in first.

" I'm sure you're right. No one could believe for a second that you were involved, and, as we know, you were staying with friends. No, Ruth will come back." She paused uncertainly. " But if she doesn't then Sir Richard will be vastly wealthy, so Nadine tells me."

" Oh?" I was on guard instantly, feeling my stomach turn over with new apprehension. " Why is that?"

I could see that Babs was watchful too. Any mention of wealth always interested her.

It was Gavin who replied.

" It's well-known. Their grandmother left her a fortune, and it was a large one, to Ruth, but if she dies before she marries and has a child then it reverts to her brother."

" Of course, Sir Richard is rich enough now." Gillian was trying Sheena's lemon cake. " He really doesn't need any more, but some men crave money, don't they, just for its own sake? Ah well! This is delicious. We're all so surprised that Sheena has proved so good a cook."

I was sick at heart. From the very moment when I had first heard that Ruth Segrave was missing, I had had a bad premonition about her. I didn't think she would come back. I don't know why, but I had been certain from the start that she had gone for good. Now Gillian and Gavin had produced a strong reason for at least one person to wish her dead. Her brother, who would inherit her fortune.

Babs put her cup down.

" She must have been a spoilt brat. I expect she was hateful."

" As a matter of a fact she wasn't." Gavin pulled a slight face, sympathising with me for having to put up with Babs. " She was very sweet, in spite of all that she had. She was modest and gentle, and we were all very fond of her."

"I doubt if I would have been." Babs bit into a cream bun as if she were sinking her teeth into Ruth Segrave. " And fancy Alex's aunt making another will in that girl's favour."

Gavin's lips tightened.

" Who told you that?"

Babs was eager now to relate the whole of the conversation with Segrave, and Gavin said tersely:

" He had no right to say such things. Alex, don't let this upset you. There's never been any proof that there was a second will."

" You knew about it?"

I was taken aback, hurt because he hadn't told me before, and that I'd had to find out from Segrave's brutal announcement.

" We all knew about it." Gavin was soothing. " At least, we all heard talk of the second will."

" Why didn't you tell me?" I could hear the tremor under my words. " Wouldn't it have been better to warn me?"

" My dear, I'm sorry." Gavin was clearly upset, moving to sit beside me on the couch. " I'm truly sorry. Yes, I suppose we should have done, but we'd no idea that Segrave would mention it. We didn't want to spoil your pleasure, that's all. We weren't trying to keep secrets from you. Damn the man! He had no right to do this."

"I'm sorry too." I could feel unshed tears hovering, hoping Babs wasn't watching me too closely. "I didn't mean to blame you, and I do understand. I wouldn't have taken this house from Ruth."

"Of course you wouldn't." He was comforting, talking to me as if Babs and Gillian weren't there. "Forget all about it. I expect your aunt changed her mind and tore the will up at the last moment. They say blood's thicker than water, don't they?"

"I shouldn't talk to Alex about blood if I were you, Mr Mortimer." Babs was licking her fingers, like a sleek, well-fed cat. "It might upset her; she doesn't like blood, do you, dear? I'm here to see that she doesn't get upset. Her mother asked me to look after her, because . . . well . . . let's leave it there. I'm to see that she doesn't become disturbed again."

I was frozen with rage, but there was nothing I could do. Babs had sowed the seed too well and even Gavin was looking at me differently. Anything I said now in protest would simply feed the fire which Babs had lit.

"I don't like talking about blood either," said Gillian after a long pause. "I don't think anyone does."

"Ah, but Alex has a special reason, don't you, darling? See, she's quite pale at the mere mention of it. I think you ought to go and lie down, Alex, don't you. We mustn't let you get distressed again."

Gavin and Mrs Baxter rose at once, the former promising to call on the following day to take me riding. I wasn't sure whether I detected something new in his expression or not. I didn't want to dwell on the possibility.

Lying on my bed, I faced the fact that I was beginning to loathe Babs. The exasperated tolerance had gone; it was quite another feeling now. She wasn't behaving like a companion at all, but like a nurse or keeper to one whose wits had gone. Also, she had said she might fall in love with Richard, and I hated her for it.

I got up, unable to rest, and wrote to my mother, filling page after page as I told her everything which had happened. When I sealed the envelope, I felt better. Writing to Lucia was like sharing my fears with her and I was buoyed up by the thought that her reply would be more bracing still.

On the landing, I met Babs.

" Are you going downstairs? If so, will you give this to Dulcie, and ask her to see that it's sent off as quickly as possible?"

" Of course." Babs was demure again. " I'll do it straight away."

I went back to my room and lay down, feeling drained of energy, but sleep proved a mistake. The dream came again and I was entombed in a dark, cramped place, knowing I would never escape; realising that I was going to die.

Then the blackness retreated and there was a girl. Although I'd never seen Ruth, I knew it was her. She was shrieking at me, calling me a thief. Then I wasn't Alexandra Leith any more, but Aunt Lucy, lying on the bed in which I was to end my days, feeling terrible pain, moaning, and breathing so deeply that my whole body shook.

I awoke with a start, perspiration on my brow. Before I could move, the whispering started, although I couldn't make out the words. Hastily, I threw the covers off and made for the window.

The trees had started to blow in the wind which had sprung up and the ivy round my window was rustling too. I was thankful beyond belief. It was the wind, as Nan had said; nothing more.

I looked round, a sudden thought striking me. There was nothing there, of course, as everyone kept telling me, but if there had been: if the room did still bear the shade of Lucinda, to whom had the dead woman been speaking? To me, her great-niece, or to Ruth Segrave to whom, so it was said, she had left the cottage in her second will?

*   *   *

Just before dinner that night, I went to Babs's room. She had borrowed the topaz pendant I wanted to wear. She had obviously gone down already, but the pendant was on her dressing-table. As I picked it up, I chanced to look down at the wastepaper-basket, bending down slowly to pick up the pieces of envelope and fragments of writing-paper.

Babs had destroyed my letter to Lucia; torn it to pieces. I felt sick once more, hurrying away in case Babs came back and discovered me there. I would have to write again, only this time I would take the letter to the village myself.

I had a feeling of utter isolation, as if I were being shut away from the real world, unable to reach out for help. Babs was trying to make people believe I wasn't normal, and certainly Gillian Baxter would have been convinced. It would be all round Winterhill and its outskirts before I knew it.

I began to worry in case Babs was right. Perhaps I was growing odd, hearing things, having awful nightmares. And I had a new fear, more chilling than any other. Segrave had implied that I had a reason to want his sister out of the way, but now I knew that he had a reason too. Maybe he wasn't as rich as Mrs Baxter thought; he could have gambled heavily and lost his money. But if Ruth died he would inherit her fortune.

Richard Segrave had a motive for murder, much stronger than mine, and I was in love with him.

*　　*　　*

I lunched with Nadine on the following day. Max, Athene, Gavin and Felix were there, the latter taking Babs's hand and making his aunt's face grow as hard as granite.

Somehow the conversation got round to Richard's visit to me and the others were as angry with him as Gavin had been.

" He had no right to say such things to you." Nadine was acid. " I really do consider it was most uncalled for. How could you have had any idea about the second will?"

" And why should he imagine you were in Winterhill the

day Ruth left?" Athene was equally put out. "You were miles away."

"I told him that, but I don't think he believed me," I replied unhappily, "but perhaps he was just worried about his sister. Is is true that she spent a lot of time with my aunt?"

"Yes." Athene nodded. "The child was always there; she loved the place."

"I can't think why." Nadine was trim and neat in blue merino and lace, her face carefully touched with powder and rouge. "Oh, how rude that sounds, but I didn't mean it that way. Frankly, I don't much care for the cottage myself."

After lunch, Gavin and I walked in the garden. He was concerned to find I'd made no attempt to get rid of Babs. I was awkward and tongue-tied on the subject, because I couldn't tell him that apart from my increasing dislike of Babs I was growing afraid of her, and the trouble she could cause.

"My mother wanted her to stay with me," I said eventually. "It's difficult."

"Don't let it be," he returned shortly. "Dismiss her straight away."

"I'll think about it again, but what could she do to me?"

I knew only too well what Babs could do, but I wanted to hear what Gavin thought. I looked at him, troubled, because I felt I was making use of his friendship. He was so kind and gentle and attentive, but he stirred me not at all.

"Almost anything." He took my arm. "Alex, do as I say; tell her to go."

"I'll try."

"Do. Have you made a will?"

I swallowed hard, feeling another spurt of fear.

"Not exactly."

"What does that mean?" His fingers tightened, almost hurting me. "What have you done then?"

"I made a promise."

"To whom?"

"Babs."

"Alex! For God's sake; what did you promise?"

"That when I die, she shall have Lucy's Cottage."

"For pity's sake, don't you realise what you've done? Can't you see that with a woman like that it's an invitation to . . ."

"To what?" I was frantic, all my self-confidence gone, my eyes filling with tears. "Invitation to what?"

"Love, I'm sorry; I'm sorry." He held me close. "I've frightened you and I didn't mean to do that, but what you've told me makes me even more certain that you should tell her to go."

He was wiping my cheek with a clean white handkerchief, his face full of concern.

"Don't you see, dearest, what a temptation that is? And Alex."

"Yes?"

I was utterly beaten. I couldn't grasp hold of my father's memory; it had eluded me. I couldn't even think of Lucia; she was too far away.

"Remember too that she won't care how she gets what she wants. Get rid of her, I beg you, before she gets rid of you."

SIX

I woke about two o'clock. I'd been dreaming again: first about Ruth and then about that lonely place where I was locked in.

I didn't want to go back to sleep for a while, in case Ruth was there, waiting for me, so I sat up to light the candle.

At first, I only heard the sound of breathing; heavy, ragged and not my own. A few seconds later the heart-beats started; steady, strong and like the tick of a clock. Finally, it was the smell, filling my nostrils and throat as I listened to the low moan of pain.

My fingers were so unsteady that I wasted three matches before the room came into view, empty, as I had known it would be. The fear was growing, but I couldn't call out for help. I just lay there, holding the sheet tightly about me, waiting for the manifestation to die away.

When it didn't fade, I managed a question in a quavering voice which I hardly recognised as my own.

" Aunt Lucy?"

Part of my mind recognised the absurdity of trying to get through to whatever was in the room with me; an old woman who had died there, but who wouldn't go away.

" Aunt Lucy, is that you?"

I half-expected a whispered reply, but at first none came. All I could hear drumming into my ears was the throb of another's heart.

" Lucy, is it me you want, or Ruth? Ruth isn't here. No one knows where she went. Do you know?"

The sudden silence was as shocking as the noises had been, and I drew back, shutting my eyes tightly. I was talking to a ghost, and that was the road to madness. People would certainly begin to believe Babs if they could hear me now.

I forced myself to drink a glass of water. A small, ordinary everyday action. It helped, for then I was able to look round again, not expecting to see anything but the outline of the furniture in the shadows.

As I blew out the candle, preparing for sleep again, I asked the question once more.

" Ruth, or me?"

To my surprise, I was overcome by drowsiness as soon as my head touched the pillow. Too many emotions; too much dread. I was mentally and physically exhausted.

At last it came, low as ever, but clear enough for me to hear even though I was drifting into slumber.

" Go to sleep, Alexandra. I'll be here. I'll always be here; waiting for you."

Not Ruth, even if a second will had been made in favour of Richard's sister, but me.

Aunt Lucinda had stayed in the cottage for me; waiting until I had come.

*   *   *

In the morning, I could hardly remember the events of the previous night. I was aware that I'd been dreaming, but the rest was blurred until the details came back to me some time later.

I told Nan and Babs that I was going to Possett's Farm to see the animals and might call on Gillian on the way back. Nan warned me about overtiring myself, but Babs wasn't interested. She was talking about retrimming a hat which she'd helped herself to the previous day.

On the way out, I met Dulcie. Surely the girl hadn't had that look at first? Sullen, yes; unfriendly, certainly. But not pert and bold. Yes, that was the word; bold. Dulcie was flexing her muscles.

I ignored her and turned in the direction of Farthing Wood, still trying to test myself. I knew it was the wrong thing to do, but I couldn't let myself be beaten without putting up some resistance.

It was the same as before. Quiet, and sombre, and lonely, and my knees began to shake as I got further into the wood. Once, I had to steady myself by holding on to an oak, but only for a second. The trunk felt cold, as if it were rejecting me.

When I heard footsteps behind me, I spun round, almost unable to stand until I saw that it was Richard Segrave.

" I'm sorry." He raised his eyebrows, obviously surprised that his appearance should reduce an apparently healthy young woman to such a state. " I'm afraid I startled you."

" It's nothing."

I managed to stand upright, controlling my voice, and my deep happiness that he was there.

" Are you sure that you're all right?"

" Perfectly, thank you. It was simply that I didn't expect to meet anyone here."

" I often walk in the wood, and so do you."

I gave him a quick look.

" Who told you that?"

He shrugged, dismissing the question as unimportant.

" I can't remember. It doesn't matter, does it?"

" No."

I tried to think of something to say, but I could do no better than make the obvious enquiry about Ruth.

" Is there any news of your sister?"

The lean face seemed harsher, the mouth harder than ever.

" None. I've questioned Simeon New again, but he can only repeat what he said before. Ruth went into your house."

" If she didn't come out, she'd still be there, and she isn't, I can assure you."

He said nothing, forcing me to continue the burden of conversation, or face a blank silence.

" She could have run into the cottage for some purpose which we don't know, and then left later, after New had gone."

I watched the hazel eyes travel over my face, my heart

leaden. For a brief moment, I'd hoped I'd been wrong about my feelings for Richard. That his arrival had coincided with a time when I was upset and frightened, and that I'd clung on to him to keep a toe-hold on sanity, but it wasn't so.

Being near to him was making me tremble, and I wanted to stretch out my arms to him and feel his body next to mine. My need for him was like a terrible thirst which couldn't be quenched. How was it possible to yearn for someone with such intensity after two brief meetings?

I remembered then that Lucia had told me she had fallen in love with my father the first second she had seen him. I had smiled indulgently at her, thinking her love was a pleasant, easy affection, but now I knew how wrong I was. I thought, too, of the morning she had come out of her bedroom to tell me my father was dead. Something had gone out of her face and it had never returned. She had loved, as I was loving now.

" If that were so, why didn't she go back to The Hall?"

The spell was broken by Ruth, and now we were walking, back the way I had come. When we reached a log across our path, Segrave held out his hand. I knew I shouldn't have taken it, but I couldn't resist. It was cool, strong and magical, and I wanted to go on holding it for ever.

"You're very pale." He released me, eyeing me again as if I were his enemy. " Are you frightened? If so, why? Is it to do with Ruth? Something you haven't told me?"

His enemy! It was ironic in a way, for I would have thrown caution and convention to the four winds had he asked me to do so. I would have become his mistress with joy and gratitude, if that was what he had wanted.

" Is it about Ruth?"

I came to earth with a bump. It was always Ruth. She stood between us like a high brick wall and we never spoke of anything else. Soon, I should start to hate her, as I hated Babs.

" No." I forced myself to be sensible. How could one hate a girl one had never met? It wasn't her fault that I'd fallen in love with her brother and was hurting all over because of it.

" How many times must I tell you I don't know anything about your sister?"

" Then why are you afraid? Don't tell me that you aren't. because I'm not blind."

I hadn't had the slightest intention of telling him about Lucy's bedroom and what I'd heard there, nor about my dread of Farthing Wood, but when he caught hold of me, pulling me round to face him, I found myself gasping out the whole story. Spoken aloud, it seemed even more ludicrous but I couldn't stop myself. The only thing I didn't mention was the blood-stained dress: I couldn't bring myself to tell Richard about that.

" And so," I ended lamely, " I think it must be that when my great-aunt died some part of her didn't go. It stayed there, in her room."

He had listened without interruption, his face quite blank. I was pleading with him to understand.

" Do you believe that it's possible? That a dead person could become part of the room in which they'd died?"

" I should think it totally impossible." His hands dropped from my shoulders. " Miss Leith, you've let that cottage get on your nerves, or, rather, what the servants and others say about it."

" But what else can it be?"

" What your maid suggested. Wind in the chimney or in the ivy. There are a number of rational explanations, but yours isn't one of them."

I flinched as if he'd hit me. I wished with all my heart that I could have taken back my words. I ought to have known that Segrave wouldn't have had any patience with such a tale; he wasn't that sort of man. I was trying to think of some way of assuring him that I wasn't as mad as he obviously thought I was, when he said:

" I hear that you've become very good friends with Gavin Mortimer." We were walking along again and he gave me a sidelong glance. " Very close, I'm told."

" You've been misinformed." I was quick to deny it, for it was of paramount importance to me that Richard shouldn't think my relationship with Gavin was anything more than mere friendship. "We ride together now and then, but there's nothing more to it than that. Sir Richard, I assure you; there really isn't more than that."

He was sardonic.

"Very well, since you tell me so with such vehemence, I believe it, but it's no business of mine. I'm not your guardian, and I wasn't suggesting that you were lovers."

I was shaken. I'd never before met anyone who spoke so bluntly, and he made me feel about ten years old.

"No, I realise that. I just wanted you to understand."

"I've told you; there's no need for me to understand. It's nothing to do with me."

I was completely crushed, the tears back again behind my lids. I wanted it to concern Richard, but, of course, he was right. There was no reason why he should be interested.

He seemed bent on hurting me, probing at the sore he'd opened.

"He's a good-looking young man; you could do worse. I'm led to believe that he's in love with you."

I stopped shrivelling before him like a beaten dog, and was suddenly and mercifully blazingly angry. I'd inherited Lucia's Latin temper, as well as her looks, and for once I was glad of it.

"Well, I am not in the least in love with him and, as you say, it is nothing to do with you. This village is so full of gossip that it can't tell truth from fiction. Please mind your own business and don't mention the subject again."

I expected a quick riposte, but to my eternal surprise I saw that he was smiling. The faint amusement brought warmth to his face and made my heart quake again. Damn love, if that was all it could do. Was there nothing to it but pain, and humiliation, and hopelessness?

He said softly:

"When you're angry, your eyes smoulder like black fire; did you know that?"

I was just aware that he'd taken my hand again, but I couldn't answer him. The good, healthy fury had died com-

pletely and I was timid and exposed once more as I savoured
each precious word.

" You are so beautiful." His voice was quieter still. " So
very beautiful."

I felt the world begin to revolve, my lips trembling. The
exact words which I'd heard once before, whispered to me
in a tone, no louder than Richard's, in an empty room.

" Good God, girl!" He put his arm round me to steady
me. " What on earth is wrong with you now? Do you always
faint when someone pays you a compliment?"

I clung to him, feeling his strength, wanting him desperately. It was so cruel that convention bound such chains
about one. If I had been a servant, Richard could have taken
me to his bed, had he wanted to do so, and no one would
have thought anything of it. As it was, we should remain
as strangers, no matter how much I needed him. In a few
months I would be back in Florence and I should never see
him again. It seemed to me to be the end of my life.

" No," I said finally. " No, I don't, but that's exactly what
the voice said. ' You are so very beautiful.' That's what Aunt
Lucy said to me."

Segrave stiffened, drawing away so that I was forced to
stand by myself. I felt very alone, and totally rebuffed, as if
he had shut a door in my face.

" Your tricks don't impress me, Miss Leith. I don't know
why you have made up this extraordinary rigmarole, or what
you're trying to hide, but you won't make a fool of me as
you have of young Mortimer. You merely make me wonder
what you are trying to conceal."

He didn't look at me again and I fell into step beside him,
tears running slowly down my face.

" I'll take you home," he said after a minute. " It's not far
now."

" Please don't trouble. I can find my own way."

" Can you?"

All I could see was a blur of tree-trunks through my
sorrow, but I didn't want help which was not freely given.

" Yes . . . I'm sure I can."

"Nevertheless, it's not my custom to leave helpless females in the depths of a wood. I shall take you back."

When I said nothing, he turned his head, and I knew he was watching me cry.

"And now tears." He didn't give an inch. "Please don't bother for me. I'm quite immune."

"Why do you hate me so?" I asked sadly as we went up the slope. "We've only just met."

"I don't hate you. I feel no emotion for you whatsoever, except perhaps some suspicion."

I wouldn't let him see the result of that fresh wound: of course he felt no emotion for me. I was a fool to think otherwise.

"I don't know what to say to make you believe me. I've done your sister no harm."

"If you are proved right, I will apologise, and most profusely."

He closed the cottage gate, making another barrier between us.

"If not, then I will know what to do with you, make no mistake about that."

I couldn't walk away yet. I stood there, an ugly thought crossing my mind. Segrave was making greatly play of his belief that I had had a hand in Ruth's disappearance, but what if that was simply to cover his own guilt? Perhaps he and his friends had been in Winterhill the night she vanished. He could have had help in removing her from his path.

"I must go in," I said at last, feeling flat and hollow inside as I thought about it. Richard and his friends: Ruth and her fortune. "They will wonder what has happened to me."

"One thing, Miss Leith."

"Yes?" I managed to look at him at last, seeing a glint in his eyes which I hadn't expected. I wasn't quite sure what it was, but it certainly wasn't dislike. "What is it?"

"The whisper, real or imaginary, was right."

"Right?"

" Yes, you are lovely; very lovely. Good-bye, and re-member what I've said. If you are not innocent, then you've made a bad enemy. I always pay my debts."

*   *   *

I don't know how I managed to sit through luncheon that day without betraying myself. I could feel, hear and see Richard in everything around me. His brief touch had brought my whole body to life; I was aware of it as never before, glad that my form was slender and well-formed, as Nan so often said to me. Even when Richard was threatening me, his voice was in my ears like music which wouldn't fade away. I longed to kiss him; to hold him in my arms.

I knew now what Lucia had suffered when she lost my father, and was ashamed of my self-centred blindness.

" Walking again?" Babs was amazed when I said that I was going out. " You'll wear yourself out with so much exercise. Where do you go, and what is there around here that's so interesting? Do you meet Gavin? Is that it? Oh, Alex, you're blushing!"

" I don't meet Gavin." I was sharper than I'd meant to be. I didn't want Gavin's name linked with mine. " I just like watching the animals on the farm, that's all."

" All right." She winked knowingly. " I won't ask again; I know how to be discreet. I shall have a rest, I think. When are you going?"

" In about an hour. Thank you, Dulcie, you may clear. Where's Miss Ponsonby?"

" Gone to Catersham with carter, Miss." Dulcie was wear-ing a secretive smile which made my nerve-ends tingle. " Needed some things, she said. Won't be back till about five."

" I have a letter to write, then I shall go, and I'm not sure when I shall be home. Just serve tea for Miss Wycombe at four, please."

" Yes, Miss."

Dulcie bobbed, struggling out with the heavy tray, fol-lowed by Babs who was yawning as if it had been she who

D

had been up at five-thirty that morning, scrubbing floors.

I went to my room, intending to write to Lucia again, but for some reason I couldn't think what to say. I sat and stared at the blank sheet of paper, until the truth dawned on me. If I told my mother what was happening, she would order me back to Florence immediately, and that would mean I shouldn't see Richard again. The day of parting would come soon enough; I couldn't do anything which would hasten it.

Thinking back to my conversation with Richard brought Gavin to mind. I felt guilty that I had pushed him out of my life so carelessly. All his kindness had been forgotten in my effort to make Segrave believe there was nothing but casual friendship between Gavin and myself.

I would have to be particularly nice to Gavin when we next met to make up for what seemed a betrayal, but not too nice. He might misunderstand, and that had to be avoided at all costs. I had to make sure that he realised there could be nothing but affection between us.

It was nearly an hour and a half before I left the house, and I didn't go to Possett's Farm after all. Almost against my will, I found myself going down to the wood, in amongst the trees which I hated so much. Why I went, I have no idea. It was as if they were drawing me in; coaxing me.

The feeling of dread soon started and it seemed very dark. I glanced at my watch. Three-thirty. It couldn't be dark yet; I would have to go back at once. Twilight in Farthing Wood was unthinkable.

When it happened, I didn't hear a thing. The first I knew was that a cloth had been flung over my head and, after that, total oblivion.

I regained consciousness nearly an hour later, my head splitting as I tugged and pulled at the thing which was covering me. It was a thick woollen shawl and I flung it aside in disgust, for it smelt of stale food and sweat.

Somehow I got to my feet, sick and giddy as I began to walk. It was very overcast and my terror was growing. Soon I wouldn't be able to see a thing and already I was hopelessly lost. I'd come further into the wood than I'd imagined and every tree looked the same. There was no path, nor track; nothing to follow back to safety.

I was afraid that I was going round in circles, for there was no sign of open country, or of the incline leading up to the cottage, and I longed for a lamp to help me find my way. I floundered on and on, stumbling, crying under my breath, head still throbbing painfully, my gown growing dirty and torn by brambles and thorns.

I was very close to collapse, about to sink to the ground and give up my efforts, when the whisper cut through my misery and defeat.

I went icy-cold, but I listened.

" Follow me," it said. " Don't be afraid; follow me. I'll take you home. I'll take you back to Lucy's Cottage."

I was like a sleep-walker, moving in the direction of the low voice which seemed to dance a few yards ahead of me. It was getting gloomier than ever, but I didn't look round. I kept my eyes straight ahead, hearing nothing but the encouraging sound which was forcing me on and on. Once, when I stopped, it grew sterner.

" Come on, come on. Don't wait here. Come home, come home."

Finally, I was out of the wood, taking unsteady steps over the brook, getting my feet soaked, but not caring at all. The dreadful wood lay behind me and I knew the way now. At the gate I paused, waiting for more words, but none came. I was uncertain again. Had they been real words, spoken softly by another, or were they simply in my own head?

It had begun to pour with rain, the heavy grey clouds which had accounted for much of the darkness drenching down. Thankfully, I reached the back door and shut it behind me.

Sheena mouthed something at me, her wrinkled face waxen, and then Nan came, taking me in her arms as if I were a child.

" Lovey, lovely, whatever's happened? Where've you been all this time? Do you know it's near to seven? We've been that worried about you."

" So late?"

I shuddered, and not just from the cold. Had it really taken that long to get away?

" Now, see, you've got a chill. Come upstairs this very minute. Girl, you and Sheena get some water boiled, and I'll put the bath out. When you've done that, come and help me get a fire going in Miss Alex's room."

I felt like a doll being undressed by Nan and Babs; the latter's stare seemed to me inimical, rather than relieved. Perhaps Gavin was right; maybe Babs wished I hadn't returned. I almost asked her whether she'd been in the woods that afternoon, but at the last second, I hadn't the courage.

" I've been to Catersham." Nan was pouring steaming water over me, sponging the aches away. " When I got back and found you weren't here, I was that feared. I sent the girl to see if you were with Miss Lancaster or the Mortimers, but they said they hadn't seen you. You shouldn't go off on your own, and that's a fact. Next time, Miss Babs or I will go with you."

I met Bab's eyes, fixed steadily on me, and felt my flesh crawl. A walk in Farthing Wood with Babs?

I had my meal in bed, not wanting food, but eating some to please Nan. She had exclaimed at the contusion on my head, assuming at once that I had fallen, and I didn't argue. It was better she thought that than learned that someone had struck me down.

I watched the fire flickering, wondering. Who would have hit me over the head and left me there, and had they thought I was dead? Was it an attempt to kill me, or just a warning?

Richard had warned me, only that morning. Surely Richard wouldn't have done this. I could feel tears close again. I had never cried as much in all my adult life as I had done since I got to Winterhill, but then I'd never been in love before, nor been so frightened.

Soon, Nan fetched my tray and kissed me good-night, ordering me not to get up the next morning until she'd had a look at me. I nodded, glad to lie in the warm bed, listening to the rain beating against the window.

I put out my hand to dowse the candle, but it was just beyond my reach. As I propped myself up on one elbow, I glanced at the opposite wall and stark fear came flooding back like a raging tide. I opened my mouth to scream, but no sound came, and then a draught from somewhere blew the candle out.

I fumbled for matches, my mind numb. The fire no longer provided any glow, for Nan had banked it up for the night, and my fingers groped helplessly over the table.

It must have been a trick of the light; I couldn't really have seen what I thought I had. A blank canvas; as empty as it had been before the artist had begun his work. It couldn't be; it simply couldn't be.

I was clumsy, knocking the clock over, my teeth chattering as finally I found the matches, dreading the moment when I lit the candle again and had to look back at that wall.

In the end, I managed to turn my head, holding myself so stiffly that I ached. The candle-stick wobbled, and I was ready to cry out, but there was no need.

The Georgian was gazing down at me, eyes gently amused as always, one slender hand on the hilt of the sword he wore. I lay back, limp as a rag. It was true what people were saying. I was letting my imagination run away with me, wrecking my nerves, and it would have to stop. My whole world was crashing about my ears and I didn't know what to do to save myself.

I wanted to stay awake, because I was afraid of sleep and what came with it, but fatigue was too great. Eyelids drooped, muscles slackened and I was floating away from reality. I was so nearly gone that the faint murmur scarcely penetrated my consciousness.

" Sleep well, my lovely, sleep well. I'll watch for you."

I knew it was just a dream, and so it was safe to smile, my lips scarcely moving as I replied.

" Thank you, Aunt Lucy, thank you. I'll rest safely now until the morning."

SEVEN

It was at Nadine's that I met Evangeline Parr. She was
exactly like a grey squirrel, even down to her smoke-coloured
paletot, finished with a rabbit-skin collar. Her hair was
pushed up into a gable bonnet, only a well-frizzed fringe
visible.

" I'm so glad you came, Miss Leith." Nadine was gracious,
presiding over the spirit-kettle. " Evangeline has been longing to meet you, for she's very interested in Lucy's Cottage."

" Oh?" I was dubious, trying not to worry about the
eagerness of Miss Parr's expression. I really didn't want to
answer a lot of questions, particularly to a total stranger.
" You knew my aunt, Miss Parr?"

" Slightly, only slightly." Evangeline spoke very quickly,
as if she were afraid she'd forget all that she had to say
unless she got the sentences out immediately. " I met her
twice when I visited with Nadine. Such a nice lady, I thought
but it was the cottage itself . . ."

I grew more uneasy still at the rapt look on the woman's
face, and Gavin gave a short laugh.

" Miss Parr is psychic. She is one of those people who can
hear and see things which others can't."

For a second, I thought Gavin was being cruel; reminding
me that I too heard things which weren't there, but the feeling didn't last. Gavin was too kind for that. He would never
say anything hurtful to me, whatever he had gleaned as a
result of Kipps's gossiping.

I smiled at him tremulously. I wanted so much to explain
to him that my fondness for him remained unaltered, despite

my feelings for Richard Segrave, but, even if we'd been
alone, I couldn't have put it into words. He wouldn't have
understood. I didn't really understand myself exactly what
Richard had done to me, simply by existing.

" Yes, my dear, I can." Miss Parr was watching me with
bright, inquisitive eyes. " I know Gavin's teasing me, because
he's an unbeliever, and I'm not sure that Nadine isn't just as
bad."

Nadine handed me a cup of tea, not letting herself be
drawn into an argument.

" I've never really thought about such things. Now,
Evangeline, do try this shortcake. It's Mrs Cameron's latest
recipe, and I know you'll like it."

"Thank you, I'm sure I will." Evangeline took a piece,
nibbling at it rapidly. " Yes, it was the cottage that I found
so fascinating. You see, Miss Leith, after your aunt died,
Nadine went there one day, just to make sure that the cook
and maid were keeping things as they should be."

" Yes." Nadine motioned Felix to pass the cakes round.
" Several of us promised the solicitor we would do that,
until you arrived."

I murmured my thanks and Miss Parr nodded.

" So wise, so wise. Servants have no conscience; none at
all, at least, most haven't. Well, as I was saying, I went with
Nadine, but at first I didn't notice anything. It was when we
got to your late aunt's bedroom . . ."

She paused to take another bite, and I grew very still, praying that no one would interrupt her, for what she had to say
was of vital importance to me, but Gavin was disposed to
joke.

" Such suspense! What was up there? A spook?"

" You mustn't poke fun." Evangeline wasn't offended,
shaking a forefinger at him roguishly. " These young men;
they don't take anything seriously, do they?"

" I take some things very seriously."

Gavin was looking at me and I knew immediately what he
meant. I prayed he couldn't read my own thoughts, and
quickly turned back to Miss Parr.

" Please go on. What did you feel?"

" Well, at first, I wasn't sure." Her biscuit was forgotten and she was no longer smiling. " I just knew there was someone there."

" Sheena, Dulcie or Nadine?"

" Now, Felix, don't you bait me too." Evangeline wasn't angry, but she was done with banter. " Of course they were in the house, but it wasn't them."

" You felt another person there?"

I leaned forward, willing the others not to speak, so that Evangeline could tell her story.

" Yes, I did. There was no mistake; there was a presence up there."

" I think this is stupid." Babs snapped off the thread. " What is the point of making Alex more nervous than she is already? We've all had enough of that kind of thing since we got here."

" Please don't interrupt." I didn't look at Babs, but for once my tone was sufficient to silence her. " Please go on, Miss Parr. What was in the bedroom?"

" Someone who was dead."

" You mean a ghost? Oh, really, Evangeline!"

" No, Nadine, I don't mean a ghost, at least, not in the way you infer."

" No white sheet, or headless maiden?"

" Gavin!" Evangeline was reproachful. " Don't make mock of things you don't understand."

" No, Gavin, please let Miss Parr go on. I want to hear what she has to say."

I was on the edge of my chair and suddenly Gavin was concerned.

" Alex, are you sure . . .?"

" Yes, I am."

He shrugged, leaning back in his chair.

" Very well, but don't blame me if you can't sleep tonight."

" I won't. Miss Parr?"

" It wasn't a ghost in the normal sense of the word." Her

explanation came tumbling out, the others quiet at last.
" Nothing to see at all, but it was there right enough. In the
room itself; the walls, the ceiling, the floor . . . oh . . .
everywhere."

" What sort of . . .?"

" Rooms retain the presence of those who have died in
them, at least some do. When the person passes over, the
bricks, plaster and wood absorb them and they stay there."

" For ever?"

I asked it in a very faint voice and saw Gavin frown.

" Mostly for ever. Of course, not everyone hears and feels
them, you understand. Only those, like me, who have the
gift."

" What did you hear and feel?"

" I heard deep, uneven breathing and a heart-beat. Later,
there was a moaning and a most unpleasant smell. Nadine
was with me at the time and I remarked upon the phenomena
but she thought me quite demented, as she always does,
because she sensed nothing."

I gave Babs a warning look, but it was too late.

" Just like Alex." Deliberately she picked out the largest
piece of chocolate cake. " We've all been driven witless by
Alex and her moans and smells."

" You too?" Miss Parr was delighted, clapping her hands
and beaming at me. " Oh, how splendid, how splendid!
Now, you're the first person I've met for a long, long time
who's receptive to such things. You heard the breathing and
the heart-beat too?"

" Yes, I thought I did, on a number of occasions, but Nan,
that is, my maid, said it was my imagination. Old houses
creaking and that sort of thing."

" Nonsense." The idea was brushed aside at once. " No,
you have the gift too."

" I think, dear Evangeline, it's time to stop this." Gavin
was watching me. " That cottage has got a bad enough name
as it is. We don't want to drive Alexandra away, do we?"

" It's all right, Gavin, I want to hear. Please go on, Miss
Parr. You really believe that when Aunt Lucinda died,

her . . . well . . . her spirit was absorbed into the room?"

Evangeline's hand was stilled in mid-air, cup poised near her lips.

"Miss Oakley? Well, I suppose it could have happened, but I doubt it."

"But I thought you said . . ."

The high-pitched laugh was like a tinkling bell, black eyes shiny as beads.

"Dear Miss Leith, it's not your late aunt up there in that room. I thought you'd realised that. It's a man."

I couldn't speak for a moment or two; it was as if all the breath had been knocked out of me. It wasn't Aunt Lucy who had spoken comforting words and promised to keep me safe; it was a stranger. I couldn't believe it. I had been so sure it was she.

"Are you certain?" I asked finally. "Are you absolutely sure it's a man?"

"Of course, and I'm never wrong about such matters. Yes, it's a man right enough, and not a good one either. You must be very careful not to offend him."

Not to offend. I felt as if every nerve in my body was twitching. Aunt Lucinda couldn't leave the cottage, in case she offended. I couldn't bring myself to move to a spare bedroom, in case I too offended.

Nadine was firm.

"That's quite enough, Evangeline. Really, you are too naughty at times. Do you want us all to have nightmares? Gavin, take Miss Leith into the library and show her those first editions which your father has just bought. I'm sure she'd be interested. And be sure to thank Max for me for letting me see them. Now, Miss Wycombe, would you like another piece of cake?"

Half-hearing the emphasis on the amount Babs had already eaten, I followed Gavin to the library, but he wasn't bothering with books, first editions or not.

"That idiotic woman!" He took my hands in his. "Dear, dear, Alex, don't look like that. It's all nonsense, you know it is."

" But I heard . . ."

" What Nan said you heard; nothing more."

" But if it wasn't? Miss Parr . . ."

" It was." He was very definite. " I could strangle Evangeline for upsetting you so. Put it out of your mind. If you've anything to worry about, it's that companion of yours. Why haven't you sent her away yet?"

" It's difficult."

" Nothing is easier. Do it soon."

" I'll think about it."

" Don't wait too long."

Babs was dismissed as his hands tightened on mine, his voice becoming a caress.

" Dearest Alex, how exquisite you are! Do you know how much I'm in love with you?"

" Gavin! Don't!"

I couldn't take it lightly and repel him gently but firmly. If I hadn't met Richard, I could have done so, but now Gavin felt like a threat to my happiness. I knew it was ridiculous, because Segrave didn't even like me, but I couldn't help myself. My rejection of Gavin had to be absolute.

He didn't mind, because he didn't know the true reason.

" Too soon? All right, I'll be patient, but be warned. I'm not easily discouraged."

I saw the tenderness in his eyes and would have given anything to be able to return what he was offering me, but there was no way I could do it. There never would be a way. I said slowly:

" Don't ask of me that which I can't give you."

" I won't, at least, not yet."

" I may never . . ."

His finger stilled my rejection.

" Never is a long time, sweetheart."

When he kissed me, I felt absolutely nothing. I was a lay figure in his arms, unmoved and untouched.

He let me go with a sigh.

" You're right, this isn't the time. Too many other things on your mind. But one day . . ."

" I must go." I made a hasty apology. " Will you say good-bye to Nadine, and thank her for me? I don't want to go into the sitting-room again."

" No, of course not. You've had enough of Evangeline for one day, and Nadine will quite understand. I'll take you home."

" Babs. I must call her."

" No." He wasn't interested in Babs. " Let her make her own way back; the walk will do her good."

" I can't just go without her."

" You can, and you will."

A maid was bringing my coat, ducking her head as she made off to the sitting-room again.

" Just one thing, Alex?"

" Yes?"

I was scared again; alarmed at the prospect of what he was going to say.

" There isn't anyone else, is there? You'd tell me if there was, wouldn't you?"

Gavin's face was no longer there, looking down into mine. Instead, I could see Richard's, every tiny detail as familiar to me as if I'd known him for years.

" Alex?"

Richard vanished and I was flustered.

" No, no, of course there's no one else."

" I'm glad. I wouldn't have liked a rival. When you've got rid of that tiresome girl, it'll just be you and me. That's how it should be, isn't it?"

" Of course," I said untruthfully, finding it even more difficult to breathe. " I really must go."

I let Gavin help me into his carriage, not understanding why his last remark had disturbed me so. I was as taut as a violin-string, sitting next to him, trying to come to terms with my new fear.

We were halfway to the cottage before it struck me. ' It'll just be me and you ' Gavin had said. It sounded as though he wanted to isolate me from other people, but he hadn't really meant it that way. It was my foolish fancies again.

And it wouldn't be just me, if Evangeline Parr was right. There would be another to share my room that night. A man; a man who was not a good one. No Aunt Lucy to promise me protection, but a dead man, who had been evil.

I smothered my exclamation of fear just in time as Gavin turned his head again to smile at me.

*   *   *

I was covering my ears with my hands, desperate to shut out the moaning, when Nan came into the room.

"Dear Lord, not again! Now, now, Miss Alex, stop that." She pulled my arms down to my sides. "We've had quite enough of this and, from what Miss Babs tells me, it's been made worse by that daft woman you met yesterday. Whatever can Miss Lancaster have been thinking about? And whatever were *you* thinking about, leaving Miss Babs behind like that? She's in a right paddy about it, I can tell you."

"Yes, I know." I loved Nan dearly, but I wished she would go away and not batter my mind with her chiding. "Do stop! I'm all right."

"So you said before, but it's not true; anyone can see that. Lost all the roses in your cheeks and some weight too, I know. Hearing things and smelling things! What next?"

"Miss Parr heard what I can hear." I moved away from Nan, putting space between us so that she couldn't over-whelm me. "It wasn't just me after all. She heard the moaning as well."

"Rubbish! She's not right in the head, that one."

"And you mean I'm not either?"

I saw Nan studying the unusual anger in me.

"No, I didn't mean that, but I do think you ought to see Dr Carlton."

"Well, I'm not going to."

My heart sank as Babs came in: was I never to be left in peace?

" So you're here." Babs was still furious. Although Felix
had driven her home, she resented my discarding her as one
of no account and was going to make me pay for it. " What
is it this time? The smell, or the heart-beat? Really, you're
as crazy as that awful Miss Parr."

" Please go away."

" Not yet." Babs held her ground, lips tight with vexation
" It's time you stopped behaving like this, or people will
really think you're mad. Perhaps you ought to go somewhere
for treatment. There are places, you know."

" How dare you?" My temper blazed so suddenly that
Nan and Babs both took a step backwards. " You are my
companion, and paid for it at that. You are not my keeper,
in spite of the lies you've told on that score, and which my
mother will hear about in due course. Go back to your own
room, and please mind your own business. You go too, Nan.
I want to be alone."

They went hastily, but at the door Babs recovered
sufficiently to say:

" Very well, Miss High and Mighty, but don't shout for
me when you next have a nightmare, will you, for I shan't
come. I hope you do see the man that wretched woman was
talking about; it would serve you right. I hope he's down-
right wicked and gives you what you deserve."

The door slammed behind her and I sank down on the
side of the bed, all my bravado gone. I needed comfort. Not
the sort which Gavin or Nan could give, but quite a different
kind. A kind I knew I should never have.

" Oh Richard," I said sadly. " How I wish I'd never met
you!"

*   *   *

After lunch I went out, because I couldn't bear the
thought of another quarrel with Babs, or a lecture from Nan.
I avoided the wood and went across the fields, weeping
inside because of a man who was scarcely civil to me.

I don't think I'd ever thought seriously about falling in

love, or, if such a thing crossed my mind, my expectations were of the most conventional kind.

Friendship first, then the dawning of a deeper feeling. Dances, and music, and gifts of flowers and chocolates. Walks together, and holding of hands. A guilty kiss now and then, and an exchange of looks which promised intimacy in time to come.

I was wry. That was what Gavin was offering me. He hadn't sent flowers or chocolates, yet the pattern was clear enough, but I'd turned him away, at least in my own mind.

I hated what love had turned out to be: it was a fraud and a cheat. Being with Richard, yet not able to touch him; talking to him, but without a word of affection exchanged; seeing him when I closed my eyes; hungering for him when I lay in bed. Despairing, because that was all there would ever be for me.

When I got back, I went up to my room. The door was slightly ajar, and I supposed it was Babs, helping herself to a trinket or blouse which she fancied. She, like Dulcie, was getting bolder; she didn't always ask now before she took my things.

When I went in, it was as if the world was splitting into fragments, making me lurch, and I should have fallen if I hadn't held on tightly to the nearby table.

I tried to pretend at first that Nan had simply fainted, but in my heart of hearts I knew at once that it wasn't so. I don't know how I walked the short distance to where she lay; I have no recollection of moving, yet I found myself staring down at her open eyes, filled with an expression I shall not forget until my dying day. There was a lot of blood, and a knife embedded in her stomach. It was driven right in up to the handle, and Nan's fingers were round it, red and dreadful to look at.

I knew I mustn't lose consciousness, for if I did I might fall and hurt Nan. It was irrational, but I couldn't injure Nan any more; she'd been hurt enough.

I will never know why I looked up at the portrait just then; nor why I found myself saying aloud:

" Did you do this?"

I nearly choked on the words. I was growing as mad as Aunt Lucinda had been. Whoever talked to a picture?

" Did you?"

I repeated it, recognising the insanity of it and the un-likelihood of a reply, so that when the answer came I began to shake like one with an ague.

" Not I, my lovely, not I. Look behind the wood."

I got to the door, though God knows how, refusing to accept what I'd heard, screaming aloud as the full horror of Nan's death finally struck home.

In spite of her threat, Babs came, and so did Dulcie, home again after the errand on which she'd been sent. She was making some excuse about the length of time it had taken, when she came into the room, but a second later she was retreating with Babs, the pair of them turning to me in un-disguised horror.

. " What's wrong with her?" Babs looked almost old. " Alex, what's the matter with Nan? What have you done?"

" Get help." I didn't even hear her question properly, or take in its implication. I just kept repeating my words over and over again. " Get help, get help, get help! For God's sake; get help!"

I don't remember anything after that. Later, Babs told everyone that I'd fainted, and I expect for once she was telling the truth.

The human mind and heart can take just so much, and I had reached my limit. Nan was dead. My dear, dear Nan, whom I'd sent away in anger.

Now, only Babs, Dulcie and a deaf and dumb old woman were in Lucy's Cottage with me. I wondered how long it would be before I was quite alone with the man who wasn't a good one.

*   *   *

Dulcie served tea in the sitting-room, snivelling as she laid the tray down in front of Nadine Lancaster.

I wasn't sure how much time had passed since I'd found Nan. It felt like a life-time, yet the hands of the clock stood at five o'clock only.

I wasn't sure, either, when the others had arrived: Max and Athene, with Gavin, who now sat beside me protectively; Geoffrey Thatcher, and Dr Carlton. Then the Baxters came, Gillian in tears, saying things to me which I hardly took in.

I was told that Dr Carlton had already had Nan's body moved and that he would see to all the details, but I still couldn't believe that any of it was real.

" I don't understand," I said, after a while. " What was Nan doing on the floor? I went in, and . . ."

" Don't." Gavin's hand closed over mine. " Dear Alex, don't upset yourself. There wasn't anything you could have done to stop her. She'd made up her mind."

I stared at him uncomprehendingly.

" Made up her mind?"

" Gavin's right." Nadine poured tea, strong with plenty of sugar in it. " Athene, pass this to Alexandra, will you? It's the best thing for shock. Yes, Gavin's quite right. There was a note, you see."

" A note?" My cup rattled in its saucer, spilling tea until Gavin steadied it. " I don't know what you mean. What note?"

Athene was soothing.

" There, there, my dear, don't look like that. It's not your fault. The note was under the body."

" I want to see it."

" I don't think . . ."

" Give it to me!"

Max shrugged at Athene's silent enquiry.

" Why not? There's no harm in that. It'll be wanted by the authorities later, I've no doubt, and she's got a right to see it."

I took the piece of paper with printed letters on it, watching them dance up and down in front of my eyes. Finally, they were still, and I could read what Nan had written.

' I can't go on. I can't forget what I saw that night we

arrived. I've tried to hide it, but I can't live any longer with such a weight on my mind.'

"Weight?" I let the note slide into my lap. "What weight? What was she talking about? Nan didn't have anything on her mind, I'm sure she didn't."

"She wouldn't have wanted to worry you." Nadine sighed and sipped her tea daintily. Even in the midst of the dire crisis, she was immaculate in pale yellow, every hair in place, face discreetly rouged. "A loyal woman, I should imagine. Not one to lay her burdens on you."

"No, she wouldn't have done that, but what could she have seen that night? Babs?"

"I don't know." Babs was quick to deny any knowledge of the matter. "We weren't together all of the time. She could have seen anything."

"Yes, but what? What could it possibly have been that would make her do this, if she did do it?"

Everyone was alert, all attention on me.

Gavin said quietly:

"I don't think there's much doubt about it. She had the knife in her hand. It was one from the kitchen drawer, so Kipps says. And the note she'd written . . . well . . ."

"No." Max was definite, putting an end to any doubts. "She killed herself right enough. After all, who else could have done it? No one was in the house at the time, I gather. You were out; Kipps was on an errand; the cook was making butter in the yard outside, and she's a harmless old soul."

"And you, Babs?"

Babs gave me a look of acute dislike.

"I went for a walk. Don't try to blame me for this."

"I wasn't," I said wearily. "I just can't believe Nan would do it. It was such a terrible way to die."

"I know, I know." Athene put an arm round me. "You'll have to accept the truth, you know, much as it hurts. Your maid must have seen something the night she got here which preyed on her mind to such an extent that finally she could bear it no longer. I know it's hard to believe in the suicide of one close to you, but there it is."

" Athene's right." The colonel was gruff, but very gentle. " It's the only answer." He cleared his throat, as if to dismiss any emotion. " Miss Wycombe, did you notice a change in Miss Ponsonby's manner of late?"

Babs looked into my eyes and I knew what she was going to do. She hadn't forgiven me for leaving her at Nadine's that day; she had never forgiven me for being who I was. Now, she was ready to take her revenge.

" Yes, I did."

I was almost ignored as the others turned to her, waiting for more.

" It was because of Alex and what she said to Nan. Hearing noises and smelling things which weren't there. Nan was worried sick. She even said she thought Alex ought to have treatment before she did someone an injury."

I quivered, but Babs hadn't finished.

" Once, Nan was on the point of confiding in me." She smoothed the folds of the shawl round her shoulders. I recognised it as one of mine; thin as a cobweb, from a famous fashion house in Paris. " It had to do with the night we got here. She'd started to say how it scared her, but then we were interrupted and, when I next asked her about it, she wouldn't say any more. Said it was best left alone, because Alex wasn't herself."

I could feel the atmosphere changing in some subtle way. The others were no longer consoling, but cautious. I could sense them drawing back, although none of them actually moved. I had to refute Babs's lie somehow, but before I could try to undo the damage Dulcie was back announcing the arrival of Richard Segrave.

Colonel Mortimer explained what had happened, but I saw the glance Richard gave me, and what little hope I had inside me was extinguished. His doubts about me were increasing; that was clear. He probably felt what the others did; that Nan had taken her own life because of a secret concerning her beloved charge. What else would drive sane, sensible Nan to self-destruction?

I wanted to get up and go to Richard; to lay my head on

his shoulder and cry and cry until I was empty of grief. Instead, I sat there, Max's voice fading from my consciousness.

What could Nan have seen that night? My visitors would obviously assume that she had seen me, when I should have been miles away. If only the McAllisters were still in England, it would have been so easy to put the matter right. As it was, they were still on their way to India, and heaven only knew when I should get a reply to my letter.

I knew where I'd been that night, even if no one else believed me, so, if Nan had seen someone, it wasn't me. Who else could it have been who would cause Nan such worry?

I raised my head, coming back to my sitting-room and my guests, finding Richard still watching me.

Richard, who it was said had been in Europe with friends. But had he been, or had it been he whom Nan had seen? If so, why hadn't she mentioned it to me? We'd always been so close, and didn't keep secrets from one another.

All at once I knew why.

I thought I had hidden my feelings for Richard so well, but I had never successfully concealed anything from Nan. She had a strange intuition where I was concerned and, although she hadn't said anything to me, she would have known exactly what I felt for Segrave and how I was suffering because of it. She wouldn't have made my agony worse for me.

Babs was speaking again and I forced myself to pay attention.

" I don't want any of you to worry." There was a new self-confidence in Babs, an assurance and authority as if she were mistress of Lucy's Cottage and not I. " I shall look after Alex, for that is why her mother sent me to England with her. She needs help, you see; she always has done. But I'm here, so please don't concern yourselves any more."

There were quiet words of approval which I scarcely heard, for I was fighting despair and a sense of helpless frustration. They all believed Babs, turning to her with relief

as she shouldered the burden of looking after the unstable
Miss Leith. Then they left, trying to smile at me. Only
Gavin stayed a minute longer.

"I'll call," he said gently. "Don't think about Nan.
Things will work out, you'll see."

Even Gavin's tone was different and I said tautly:

"But Babs. . . ."

He looked more perturbed than I'd ever seen him look
before.

"Yes, I may have been wrong about her, after all. I know
I told you to send her away, but you can't be alone, now that
Nan's . . . She isn't quite what I thought, and you do need
someone here to look after you."

"But you said that Babs hated me; that she meant me
harm!"

"I know, I know." He comforted me quickly, looking
over to the door where Babs was graciously saying farewell
to the colonel. "I think I was mistaken. She has stepped
into the breach very well. You'll be all right."

"Gavin!"

But he was moving away, following his father out.

"Sir Richard!"

Babs was brisk and well pleased with herself.

"He's gone, Alex. Now, don't make a fuss. You've had
enough attention paid to you for one day. You'd better go
and rest, while I give Sheena and Dulcie orders about dinner.
Off you go."

"I don't want to rest!" I was fighting the pressure which
Babs was exerting, but I knew that I was losing. "I want to
talk to Sir Richard."

"I've just told you; he's left." Babs was smiling and I
shuddered. "They've all left, Alex dear. Apart from Dulcie
and Sheena, it's just you and me now; just you and me."

EIGHT

Richard called again the next morning. It was Babs who received him, pouring coffee and smiling brightly in my direction.

"Miss Leith had a good night. I thought it wise to give her a draught with her hot milk. I didn't want her to lie awake fretting."

I took my cup, feeling like a tiresome child in the charge of a patient, long-suffering governess. So that was why my head ached so and why I had had such a foul taste in my mouth. Babs had taken it upon herself to drug me without my knowledge, but then she was assuming more power with each hour that passed.

"No doubt." Segrave dismissed any grief I might have felt for Nan with a disinterested glance in my direction. "I had no opportunity of talking to Miss Leith yesterday afternoon, but there is a question I want to ask her."

"Well, I don't know." Babs was very much in control. "I don't want her worried in her present state. Couldn't it wait?"

I sat there as mute as Sheena, praying that Babs would go, and that Richard and I could talk, even if it was yet again about his sister. I couldn't think what had happened to me since I'd arrived in Winterhill. Where had all my self-confidence gone; my natural, easy authority over my staff? People tended to call me determined, when what they really meant was pig-headed, yet there I sat, allowing my companion to decide what I should do, humbly praying that she would relent and let me be with Richard for just a little while.

" No."

If I had become a mouse, Segrave certainly hadn't. He ignored Babs as if she weren't there, and I was torn between happiness and pain as he turned to me.

" Miss Leith, are you quite certain that your maid never gave you a hint of what she saw that night? Didn't she say anything which you might not have thought important at the time, or perhaps have forgotten? Please think hard."

" Sir Richard." Babs was very upright, piqued because he wasn't responding to the role she had elected to play. " Please don't pester Miss Leith. I can't let you upset her."

His hazel eyes, cold and brilliant as jewels, turned in Babs's direction, and I looked at her too. Her hair was arranged differently and she had on a new dress of mine, green surah, with a cuirasse bodice, which I'd bought in Rome and never taken out of its box. She must have worked hard the previous night to let the seams out, and I shrank back in my chair. She was taking me over, and all my possessions too, and yet I seemed helpless to stop her.

" Miss Leith?"

Segrave's attention was on me again.

" No." I managed to speak at last. What must he have thought of me, letting a servant dictate to me in that way? As I looked at him, I was already mourning. Very soon, whatever happened, we should be going our separate ways. Talking to Richard now was all I would ever have of him, and even that Babs was spoiling. " No, I'm sorry, I can't remember a thing."

" You'll have to forgive her." Babs was smooth, butting in again. " Under such a strain, you know. She hardly remembers anything properly now."

" That's not true!" My denial was feeble, but I had to attempt to fight back, or go under for good. " I remember things perfectly well."

" Like sounds which aren't there?"

" I'd like you to go." I knew there was no hope, but I had to try. " I want to speak to Sir Richard alone."

" I dare say you do, but that isn't possible. I'm afraid I

shall have to ask you to leave, Sir Richard. As you can see, Alex is becoming agitated, and I can't let that happen. I'll ring for the maid."

For a moment, I thought Richard was going to stop Babs; to insist that she left, but in the end he rose and I slumped back, defeated, as he followed Dulcie out.

" I'm sorry about that." Babs poured herself another cup of coffee, generous with the cream. " I shall give Kipps orders that he's not to be admitted again."

" You won't!" My anger was a frail thing, and I knew Babs wouldn't take any notice, but the thought of Richard being shut out was too much to bear. " This is my house, and I'll say who shall visit me and who won't."

" Not for a while." Her eyes were like pebbles, beating down my resistance. " Not until you're well again, if, of course, you do get well again."

" There's nothing wrong with me! Stop it, Babs, stop it! Oh, don't. . . ."

I dissolved into tears and Babs smiled, satisfied now that she'd scored.

" There, there, it's just what I said would happen. That wretched man's upset you. Off you go to your room, and rest."

" I don't want to."

The arm which forced me out of the chair was surprisingly strong. I'd never associated Babs with physical strength before, but I was powerless in her grip.

Upstairs, I began to think again about Evangeline Parr's assurance that it wasn't Lucinda I could sense. Certainly, I'd never been able to tell if the voice was male or female, but I'd been so sure that it was my aunt. She had told George Carlton that she wouldn't leave the cottage after her death; she had whispered that she would protect me.

But if such phenomena were true at all there could be more than one spirit trapped in the fabric of Lucy's Cottage: my aunt, and Evangeline's man, who wasn't a good one.

Miss Parr hadn't mentioned the whisper; only I had

heard that, so the possibility of two separate persons, now dead, was quite feasible. Yet, if Evangeline had been wholly right, who was the man? Automatically, I looked at the portrait, feeling chilled to the bone. He had probably lived in the house once: that was why his portrait was there. He could easily have died in the bed in which I now slept. Breathing and heart-beats were common to all mortals and, if he'd died in pain, he could have moaned too.

It was beyond doubt that he had a wicked air about him. I suspected he'd been a rake; young, wild, uncaring, and that his beauty was only skin-deep.

I was glad when it was time to go downstairs again so that I didn't have to think about him any more. Babs was waiting for me.

" Lunch-time, Alex. I've told Sheena to get a hot meal. I don't really like a cold repast. All right for the servants, but not for us. Go back and wash your hands, there's a good girl."

She waited for me to dispute the point, but I didn't. Like a small child, I went back to my room, pouring water into the china bowl on the wash-stand.

As I dried my hands, I suddenly thought of what I'd heard the afternoon I'd found Nan dead. When, in a moment of utter lunacy, I'd asked a piece of painted canvas if it had killed my maid, the answer had come back: ' Not I, my lovely, not I. Look behind the wood.' I had forgotten all about the instruction in my grief and growing fear. My mind was swamped with other matters, not least my hopeless love for Richard.

I hated the thought of going into Farthing Wood again, but it had to be done. Perhaps all the answers were to be found there: I would have to go and see.

I hardly touched my food, watching Babs stuff herself, going submissively to my room to rest, at Babs's suggestion, which was no suggestion at all, but an order.

When I was sure Babs was sleeping off her heavy meal, I crept downstairs. The sun had gone in and, when I stepped across the stream, Farthing Wood was more formidable than ever, but it had to be faced. Even a hint, or slight clue, would be worth the ordeal and I tried not to look behind me as I hurried on.

I was out of breath when I reached the far end, but I forced myself to go further, into the meadow beyond, so that I could look back and see clearly what was behind the wood.

I felt moisture blurring my vision. There was nothing behind Farthing Wood; nothing at all. The journey had been fruitless and, if the place held any secrets, it wasn't revealing them to me.

I dreaded going back, but the long way home would have meant that I should be very late and Babs would be furious. Babs furious! I straightened my shoulders, cowardice finally falling away from me like a discarded garment. Let Babs be furious. I was the mistress, she the servant, and I would make that plain immediately I saw her.

She was in the sitting-room, wearing a modest little frock she had made herself. She smiled at me; welcoming me home.

" Just in time, dear. Sheena's made some delicious scones. Do try one. You ought to eat, you know."

I gritted my teeth to stop them chattering with nerves. Babs wasn't angry; she wasn't domineering either. She was just as she had been when we had first arrived in Winterhill, and I had to clench my hands tightly by my side to stop myself from screaming.

Had I imagined what Babs had been like that morning? I was shaken by self-doubts, terrified that the thing in Lucinda's bedroom, and the death of my dear Nan, had really affected my mind.

I decided to test Babs; to make sure which was the real one.

" Babs?"

" Yes?"

" The dress that I bought in Rome: the green surah."

" Yes?"

" Do you know where it is?"

She looked at me in surprise, munching away at Sheena's scones spread thickly with home-made jam and cream.

" No, I don't think I've ever seen that one. What's it like?"

" I thought . . ."

" Yes, dear?"

I couldn't go on. I made an excuse and went upstairs, feverishly searching in the wardrobe. Then I saw the box on the floor; white, with gold lettering, and a red and gold emblem. I tugged the lid off, almost tearing the tissue paper in my frenzy. The gown was there, neatly folded, as it had been on the day it was purchased.

I considered the possibility that Babs was playing a devious game for some purpose. I had been so sure she'd had the dress on that morning. I wondered whether to ask Kipps, but decided against it. Kipps wasn't to be trusted to tell the truth.

I got up, the dress-box forgotten, turning to my Georgian.

" There wasn't anything there: behind the wood, I mean. Nothing at all."

I was talking to a picture again. Oh yes, I was becoming odd; bereft of my senses as Lucy had been. The painted mouth was more mocking than ever, as if he thought me a fool, which I was. I said slowly:

" How I wish you were alive and could talk to me! Oh God, I do feel so alone."

*   *   *

Dulcie brought my hot milk at ten o'clock. I had gone to bed early, too tired to stay and listen to Babs's chatter as she worked on a piece of embroidery.

" 'Ere you are, Miss." Kipps was smiling, just as Babs had smiled that morning. " Drink up every drop, Miss Wycombe says."

I didn't move, wondering whether the girl's grin was really like Babs's satisfaction earlier that day, or whether it was another quirk of my disturbed mind. I ought to have moved from Lucy's bedroom; it was insane to remain there and let it destroy me.

Dulcie's hand was still outstretched and finally I reached for the glass. Before I could take it, there was an ear-splitting crash, and Dulcie yelled aloud, dropping the tumbler on the bedside table, splintering it into pieces.

" Gawd!" She was ashen. " The picture; it's fallen orf the wall. That means a death. Oh, Gawd 'elp me, someone's goin' to die."

She fled, leaving me looking at the blank wall. Finally I got up, avoiding the broken glass, and went to inspect the picture. The cord wasn't frayed; it had snapped for no apparent reason. Yet no harm had been done. The portrait was undamaged; even the frame had withstood the shock.

Babs came in clucking.

" That stupid girl's having hysterics. Talking about a picture and a death. Whatever have you been doing now, Alex?"

" Nothing." I got back into bed, so that Babs shouldn't see how I was shaking. " I did nothing. The picture simply fell, that's all."

Babs was unconvinced, and also critical again.

" I can't imagine how you can stay in this room, after finding Nan here. All that blood Kipps had to scrub away. It shows that you're not yourself. Anyone else would have moved out at once; I know I would."

" I can't leave this room."

" Whyever not?"

I hesitated. I didn't really know why not: I just knew I had to stay. Everyone had tried to persuade me to move: Nadine, Athene, Gavin and Babs, but I'd refused. I had to remain where I was, as Aunt Lucy had had to. I couldn't offend.

Offend. My mind was racing. Kipps had said there was something in the house which wouldn't let Lucinda go, and which she couldn't offend. That bore out Evangeline Parr's theory of some presence other than Lucinda in the room. Someone who had died before my aunt.

" Alex?"

I came back to the present with a bump, finding Babs frowning.

" I'm all right," I said hastily. " It doesn't worry me here."

" Then you're either very brave, or out of your mind."

She wasn't in a hurry to go, curling up on the end of the bed as she so often did.

" It's a good thing I'm here, isn't it, now that Nan's dead?"

I tried to pay attention to her.

" Yes, I suppose so."

" Of course it is." She was very emphatic, willing me to agree. " You wouldn't like to be left here with only Sheena and Dulcie. You need someone to talk to. I have to stay to help you; I can't desert you now."

I wondered what Babs would say if I'd told her that I had been talking to a painting of a man long dead, but I didn't risk it.

" Yes, I suppose you're right."

" Good, because I don't want to go home yet. I love it here. You haven't changed your mind, have you?"

My attention was wandering again.

" Alex!"

" Yes, yes. What about?"

" Leaving the cottage to me when you die."

" No, but I don't want to talk about death tonight."

" Dulcie says someone will die, because the picture fell."

" Well, it won't be me." I felt repugnance run through me again at Babs's greed. Avarice and insensitivity: perhaps I'd have been better off with Sheena and Dulcie, but it was too late now.

When she finally went, I lay awake for a long time. Did Babs change from her normal frivolous self, to a determined gaoler, or did I imagine it? I couldn't be sure. I couldn't be sure of anything any more.

In the early hours of the morning, when everyone was asleep, except me, I thought about Richard, and there were tears on my cheeks. Perhaps unrequited love sent one mad. It was my first experience of that unhappy state and so I didn't know what dire effects might follow. All I knew was that I loved Richard so much that it was like a sickness. I hoped I'd dream of him, but, when I finally dropped off, it was Ruth I saw, calling me a thief and a murderess.

A thief, because I'd got the cottage she longed for, but a murderess? I sat up in a cold sweat, still hearing the screeching in my ears.

How could anyone kill a girl they'd never seen, and no one was yet sure that Ruth was dead.

Then I remembered the blood-stained dress and prayed harder than I'd ever done before.

" Oh, dear God, don't let it be Ruth's blood! Don't let it be Ruth's."

*   *   *

Gavin took me riding the next morning. I waited until we were resting on Haverill Rise before I broached the subject.

" Gavin, what do you think happened to Ruth Segrave?"
He shrugged.
" It's hard to say. Why do you ask?"
" I just wondered what you thought."
" Well, as the others do; that she ran away."
" But why should she?"
" There could be any number of reasons which we don't know about, but there isn't any other answer, is there?"
" She could be dead."
" In that case, her body would have been found. Alex, I don't think that you ought to dwell on such things; it's morbid. Segrave's home now; let him find her."
" I can't think why he hasn't been in touch with the police."
" He has, or so Nadine says. Abe Benson heard from one of the servants at The Hall that Segrave had gone to Shottley to talk to them."
I held my breath.
" What did they say?"

" I've no idea." He was dry. " Segrave would hardly tell me, but if servants' gossip is to be relied upon they too think she ran off."

" Won't they come here and question people?"

" I doubt it. What would be gained by that? What could we tell them that we haven't already told Segrave?"

" I thought the police always investigated when someone disappeared."

" Only if the circumstances are suspicious, or foul play is feared."

" And they don't think there's anything unusual in the way Ruth went?"

" Obviously not. Now, I'm going to take you home; you've been out long enough."

" I'm not an invalid." I was vexed as he helped me up. " I haven't been ill."

" No, but you've had a bad shock and that can be worse than physical illness. You need to be taken care of."

" By Babs?"

I was caustic and he laughed.

" Not for much longer."

" What does that mean?"

He tilted my chin, looking at me with love.

" I'll tell you soon, but not until you've got over Nan."

I stiffened. Gavin wasn't talking about Babs or Nan, but about himself, and I didn't want to hurt him.

" Gavin, I ought to tell you . . ."

" Not today."

" It's important that you shouldn't think . . ."

It was useless; he wouldn't let me go on.

" Another time, my sweet. There's no hurry, is there?"

As we rode home, I found myself thinking about Farthing Wood again. Perhaps it was because I could see it, over to the west. It was sinister, even from that distance. What had those words meant? ' Look behind the wood.'

If I had picked up an echo from the past, like Evangeline Parr could do, surely it had to make some kind of sense. Why had I been told to look there?

The answer which flashed into my mind was so ghastly that I was thankful Gavin was ahead of me and couldn't see my face.

Perhaps the voice hadn't been talking about Nan at all, as I had first thought, but about Ruth Segrave.

There was no actual proof that Richard had gone to Shottley to see the police. He might have told his servants that that was what he'd done; it would have been expected of him. He might also have told his staff that the authorities couldn't help, since there was no reason to think that Ruth had gone, other than of her own free will.

And, if he'd lied, was it because he already knew where his sister was? A fake journey to Shottley, which everyone accepted without question, confirming the common view the girl had run away.

I was completely dead inside, the vision of Richard's face so clear that it blotted everything else out.

Ruth could be lying behind Farthing Wood, buried there by her brother, who would get her fortune. Only I had heard the instruction to look beyond the trees, and no one else would even think of searching for Ruth in such a place.

She would stay there for ever, until the earth had consumed her flesh, and her bones had become brittle with age.

No one would ever know.

NINE

As I undressed, I looked at the portrait once more. He just smiled, as he always smiled, and I lay down, waiting for sleep to come. I hadn't drunk my milk. Insomnia was better than one of Babs's draughts and, although she was her usual self that day, I was taking no chances.

The hours wore on, yet I remained awake. Two o'clock struck on the longcase clock in the hall and then, quite suddenly, I knew I wasn't alone any more.

"Not her own hand, my lovely, not hers. Look elsewhere in Winterhill."

Aunt Lucy, or Evangeline's wicked man? I simply didn't know. I lit the candle at once, but, as usual, there was nothing to see, yet the presence was strong.

"What do you mean?" I was as hushed as my ghostly companion, whoever it was. "Are you saying that Nan didn't kill herself?"

I waited, but there was no answer, and I was left with the chilling thought that if what I'd heard was true someone in Winterhill had murdered Nan. And, if they'd done that, had they also killed Ruth Segrave? Whoever stabbed Nan must have believed that she'd seen someone that night when Ruth vanished. To silence her, they'd ended her life.

One by one the faces of my new friends and acquaintances came before me, but I simply couldn't believe any of them guilty of putting another to death. They weren't that kind of people. They were ordinary, normal, kindly, for the most part, showing no sign of keeping so deadly a secret. Surely none of them was the consummate actor, or actress, they would have had to be to conceal what they'd done?

E

But Richard. I closed my eyes. It was only too easy to imagine him removing from his path anyone who might be a danger to him, and he had such a strong reason for wanting his sister dead.

I thought about it harder, hating myself. If Simeon New had really seen Ruth go into the cottage that night, he might not have waited long enough to see Richard, and perhaps his friends, follow her in. If he and his companions had killed Ruth, was it possible that they'd left something behind them which would betray them? I hadn't seen anything myself and Kipps hadn't mentioned finding an object which couldn't be explained, yet it was a possibility which couldn't be discarded entirely. Perhaps one of them had gone back to find whatever it was, and Nan had disturbed them, and died for it.

I was so wrapped up in my worry and grief about Richard that I hardly heard the answer to my question when it came.

" Oh, please!" I was distraught, in case I was too late. " I didn't hear you. Aunt Lucy, or whoever you are, what are you saying?"

Another slight pause and then the reply once more.

" Make them show themselves."

I wasn't dreaming : I was wide-awake, every nerve straining.

" How?"

" Tell them you know who your maid saw. Then you'll learn the truth. Tell them."

The silence which fell was total and I knew that I was alone again. I lay back, frightened and unsure. Tell them? Gillian was having a dinner-party the next day. Everyone would be there, even Richard, she had been proud to announce. It would be an ideal opportunity to say what I'd been told to say, but it would also mean that I should be giving myself away to the killer, if a killer there was. Somehow I knew that the voice hadn't been talking about the villagers, or a stranger. The people I was told to inform about my false knowledge was one of the circle I now moved in.

I felt cold; colder still inside. It wasn't the risk of alerting a murderer which was making my heart like lead, but the possibility, or more likely probability, that the man concerned was Segrave.

I knew then what was meant by heart-break. It wasn't just a thing one read about in books, or a casual phrase, lightly used. It was a tearing, all-consuming agony, for which there was no cure.

"Oh Richard!" Even in the darkness I could still see his face. "Dear God, my love, don't let it be you."

*   *   *

The next morning it was Babs who brought my tea in, highly indignant.

"Would you believe it?" she said, pulling the curtains back with such vigour that the wooden rings clattered like drum-beats. "That sly cat, Dulcie, has gone."

"Gone?" I was drugged with sleep. It seemed only an hour ago since I had dropped off. "Gone where?"

"I don't know." Babs handed me the cup. "All her things have gone too; not a stitch left up in her room. Drink that do, Alex, and then get up. I simply don't know what we're going to do with just Sheena to clean and cook."

"Perhaps she'll come back."

In a way, I hoped that Dulcie had gone for good, no matter how inconvenient it was. There had been a certain gloating triumph in her manner of late which I hadn't liked.

"If she'd meant to return, she'd hardly have taken her clothes with her, would she?" Babs was waspish. "I expect she's making for London; that's where they all go."

"They?"

"Girls like her, and they all end up on the streets. Well, are you going to get up?"

"Yes, of course." I was almost apologetic for Babs's spell of meekness appeared to have passed. She was being mistressy again. "Don't worry about the cleaning; I expect we can get some girls from the village."

Her laugh was scornful.

"My dear Alex, you can be quite brainless at times. No one will come to Lucy's Cottage from the village, you know that perfectly well. They're far too afraid of it."

"Well, what are we going to do? Sheena can't manage everything."

"I don't know yet, but I'll tell you this now. You won't get me scrubbing floors and polishing."

"I haven't asked you to do so."

The brief return of my spirit made Babs toss her head, but her irritation was of short duration and she was smiling in a way which brought all my fears back.

"I don't suppose Sheena will stay long either." She was tracing a pattern with her finger along the side of the tallboy. "Then it will be just you and me, like I said. You're almost alone now, Alex, dear. Isn't it a good thing I'm with you?"

There was an undertone of menace in her words and I was all fingers and thumbs as I washed and dressed. I hated to admit it, but Babs was right.

I was almost alone in Lucy's Cottage.

*　　　*　　　*

The Baxter's party was going well. Gillian was beaming with pride at her well-set table, and her triumph at getting Richard Segrave to accept her invitation was clear. She had pulled off a near miracle and was preening herself because of it.

I wondered why Richard had agreed to come, for he was known to be unsociable, and the Baxters were the last kind of people I imagined he would seek for company.

I found myself in a group with Max and Athene. Max was affable as usual, a glint of admiration in his eye.

"You look charming, m'dear, quite charming. Thought any more about selling the cottage? Athene told me she'd mentioned the possibility to you."

"No, I haven't really given it proper consideration." I didn't want to refuse outright and offend the Mortimers, so

I took the coward's way out and played for time. "Nan's death . . . you know."

"Naturally." Max was still benign. "Quite understandable, and I shouldn't have worried you about it yet, but when you're more yourself . . ."

"Yes, I'll let you know."

I was glad when they began to talk to Nadine and Felix, so that I could relax and not watch every word I said.

When Richard came up to me, I was almost trembling with excitement, but I was afraid too. He wasn't admiring, as Max and Gavin had been: he was as bleak as a winter's day.

He took me on to the terrace. The night was warm and the French doors leading from the drawing-room were open. I could smell late roses in the beds just below us and my heart contracted. Roses were my favourite flowers and I had always promised myself that when I married I would choose them for my bouquet. Now, of course, I would never marry.

"Your companion tells me that Kipps has gone." He was weighing me up again. "Do you know why?"

"No, I don't. I've no idea."

I had to look away, because I was afraid he would see in me my fear of his guilt, but he misread my evasiveness.

"You don't seem to me to be very open, Miss Leith."

He was so close to me that I could hardly keep still.

"Whenever we talk, I sense that you're holding something back."

"I'm not, truly I'm not." I sounded like a skivvy being reprimanded, and cursed myself for not being able to stand up to him. Did love always make people so craven, or was it only me who was thus afflicted? "When I do tell you anything, you don't believe me."

"All that nonsense about moans, and heart-beats? Well, you can hardly blame me for that."

"It wasn't . . . isn't . . . nonsense." I almost hated him for a moment for not caring how miserable and scared I was. "It's the truth."

" I doubt it, and you're not being honest with me now, are you? What is it you're hiding?"

Then I did look at him and grew slightly giddy as he raised his hand and laid it very gently against my cheek. So deep was the effect of his touch on me that I almost gave in. Another second or two and I should have told him I knew he'd killed his sister for her money, but that I didn't care. I was saved, because the gong for dinner sounded at that moment, and I said quickly:

" We must go in."

" Yes, but before I'm done with you you'll tell me the truth."

He bent his head and, incredibly, our lips were touching. He didn't seem to mind whether anyone in the room behind us was watching, and neither did I.

His kiss was nothing like Gavin's had been and I was no lay figure this time. I had no idea why Richard had pulled me close to him; I just knew that it was the most wonderful moment of my life and that it would be the only time I should ever be in his arms. I responded with every part of me; hungrily, passionately, gratefully.

When he released me, he was smiling very slightly, but at first I was breathless and overcome with confusion and shame. The witchcraft had gone and we were two ordinary people again: visitors in Gillian Baxter's house. Only a harlot kissed a man who wasn't her husband like that, and, in my case, the sin was worse, for I believed him to be a man who had taken life, for gain.

But then, under the guilt, I was exultant. For a few seconds he had been mine and, whatever he had done, I wanted him. Wanted him to make love to me, fully and completely, no matter what the consequences might be.

I was glad that I wasn't sitting near him at table, for I couldn't have stood the burden of polite small talk. Trivial things had no part to play between Richard and me.

The others had heard about Kipps's flight too and Athene was sympathetic.

" What a nuisance for you, and only poor old Quinny left

to cope. We'll have to try to find help for you. Gillian, don't
you know anyone?"

Mrs Baxter looked doubtful.

"I know a few girls in need of positions, but I doubt
whether they'd want to . . ."

"No, quite." Nadine was severely practical. "You won't
get anyone to work in that house, I'm afraid. I suppose you'll
go to London, Miss Leith, until it's time to return to
Florence."

"No, I can't do that."

I could feel everyone looking at me, and coloured up
again. I must have sounded too emphatic to a perfectly
reasonable question, but help came from a surprising
quarter.

"I'll send you a girl." Segrave was considering me
thoughtfully over the rim of his glass. "There's no need
for you to leave."

"Surely your maids won't want to go to Lucy's Cottage
either?" Nadine seemed put out by his intervention. "They'll
be just as reluctant as the others."

"They'll do as I tell them," he returned smoothly.
"Don't worry, Miss Leith. I'll attend to it in the morning."

I wasn't sure that I wanted one of Richard's maids in my
house, running back to him every so often to report on my
doings, but I could hardly say so. I thanked him, wondering
why it had gone so quiet, as if Gillian's guests thoroughly
disapproved of the plan.

But the silence passed and talk became general again. It
wasn't until we were finishing the meal, that I summoned up
sufficient courage to do what I'd come to do.

"I think I know who Nan saw that night."

The effect of my bald announcement was as catastrophic
as I knew it would be. There wasn't a movement round the
table; not a rustle of a napkin, nor chink of silver against
porcelain. The stillness was wholly unnerving and I shall
never know how I managed to look at each of them in turn.

All I was conscious of were eyes: pair after pair, staring
at me. I couldn't be sure whether I could read guilt in any

of them or not, but after a moment I could sense a threat from somewhere. It was intangible, impossible to pin-point, but I knew it was there. Perhaps Evangeline Parr had been right, and I had a gift which most other people didn't have. All I was certain about was that I'd just put my head in a noose.

I gave a brief laugh which wasn't quite steady.

"I shall take a draught when I get home," I said at last, knowing I had to finish my task. "I must get a good night's sleep, if I'm to go to Shottley to see the police in the morning."

It was Athene who asked what everyone else wanted to know.

"How can you possibly be sure?" She was short with me. "You weren't here that night, and, if you had found out, why didn't you say something when your maid killed herself?"

"I didn't know then, but I do now, and I'm afraid I can't explain. I must talk to the police first. Mrs Baxter, I'm sorry if I've spoilt your party, but I thought I ought to tell you all what I was going to do."

"Nothing to forgive." Gillian was flustered and upset. "Shall we leave the men to their port?"

The atmosphere in the drawing-room was arctic. The others kept well away from me, talking together, casting me a glance every now and then which told me plainly that I was an outcast.

Only Babs spoke to me.

"Are you making it up, Alex?" She had brought my coffee over and when I looked at her I couldn't read her expression. "I don't believe you've any idea."

"I have. I do know."

"Then tell me at once."

The round eyes looked more than ever like my china doll's: blank and glassy.

"I can't." I began to edge away. "I can't tell anybody; it wouldn't be safe."

The rest of the evening was full of unease and I was

thankful when it was time to go, but another problem
awaited me. Abe Benson and his gig hadn't arrived to take
Babs and me home.

" I'll drive you." Richard stepped into the breach before
Gavin could open his mouth, doubtless to offer the same
service. " It's no trouble; if you are ready?"

If Babs hadn't been with us, I'm sure Richard would have
questioned me. The look he gave me as he helped me into
the carriage was hard to interpret. Coldness, certainly, and
some anger, but there was another emotion there, even worse.

For once, I was glad my companion was with us. It would
probably be Richard's eyes I should see again later that night;
his touch I should feel, not gentle this time, as it had been
earlier in the evening.

I was drained as we went into the cottage, having watched
the carriage go. Babs had gone to the kitchen to get our
nightcap, and I sat in my bedroom, as nervous as a kitten.

" I expect he'll forget all about sending us help," said
Babs as we drank our milk. " I don't think I want anyone
from The Hall here anyway."

I hadn't the courage to remind her that it was my business
to decide who worked at Lucy's Cottage and who didn't. It
might not be Segrave's eyes I should find fixed on me later,
but a pair of blue ones borrowed from a toy.

At last Babs rose.

" I'm going to bed. I shall sleep like the dead, and without a draught." The smile on her lips made my heart jump
into my mouth. " Have you ever thought what it would be
like to be dead, Alex? It must be so cold under the earth,
don't you think?"

She was gone, taking one of the lamps with her, whilst I
put a shawl over my flimsy dress and sat down to wait for
whoever was coming to end my life.

*   *   *

Nearly four hours later, I was still sitting on the side of
the bed, my limbs stiff, my mind numb. I wondered whether
I had been completely wrong about everything. The words

could have been in my head, and not real at all. Perhaps Nan really had committed suicide and maybe Ruth Segrave had run away after all.

The whole bubble of fear round me could have been self-induced, and my neighbours could be quite innocent, and shocked to find they had another Aunt Lucy in their midst.

I was about to venture down to the kitchen to make tea, when quite suddenly my skin started to crawl, as if a million tiny insects were walking over it.

" Not Farthing Wood, my lovely; you looked in the wrong place."

Slowly, I turned my head and looked at the portrait, raising the candle so that I could see it more clearly. Then my eyes moved upwards and hot wax fell on my hand as it shook like an old woman's.

The shadow was life-size, where the picture had once hung. A silhouette, misty in the half-light, but clear enough to see the outline of a powdered wig, a perfect profile, and even delicate lace at the wrists.

" No!"

I said it loudly, but then I heard footsteps and the shadow was gone in an instant.

" Babs?"

I couldn't move. I just stood there and waited as the door began to open.

" Babs, answer me! Is that you?"

I knew there wouldn't be a reply. Whether the voice was in my head or somewhere in the bedroom, it had been right. What I had said at Gillian's dinner-table had brought someone to my door. My folly in listening to the whisper was going to cost me my life.

It is strange how many things can pass through one's mind in the space of a few seconds. As I watched the gap of the door widening, my thoughts were of Richard, and the way we had kissed. I felt no regret about that; I was only sorry that he had never been completely mine, and now he was going to destroy me.

The tall figure which came through the door wore a dark cloak and it was obvious that there was a scarf or something similar covering the face, only the eyes catching a gleam of the candle's flame.

I had seen those eyes before: they were familiar, and my heart sank.

" Richard? Oh, my dear, I prayed that it wouldn't be you. Did you kill Nan as well as Ruth? I suppose it was you Nan saw that night, and you were afraid that eventually she would tell me."

He moved nearer to me and I could see the knife, held firmly in a gloved hand. I was rigid with terror, but there was worse to come.

As I began to back away, I heard a noise behind me, turning sharply. The panelling beyond the four-poster had slid open and there was the dark, enclosed space of my nightmare. At least one question had been answered. I had dreamed of the future, not of the past, and here was my grave, waiting for me.

Yet in my dream there had been more than one person. At least two had lifted me into the place where I was to die. I didn't think the horror could grow deeper, but when I saw Richard in the opening it was as if I were already dead. The other man must have been one of his friends. It was all falling into place now, and I had been right. Richard had killed his sister, and his friends had helped him. First Ruth had to go, then Nan and now me.

Then I saw something lying on the floor beyond the panelling. A shapeless bundle, lit faintly by the candle Richard was holding. Although I wanted to run away, and never know the final truth, I found myself walking forward.

My mind was telling me that when I reached the panel, I should die, for that was what I had first dreamt, but my eyes were registering a sight so awful that I had to cling to the bed-post for support.

A young girl, probably pretty when she had been alive. There was a savage wound in a stomach, and a lot of blood, long dried. The smell was appalling, for the corpse was beginning to decompose, and I wanted to retch.

"Your own sister." I tore myself away from the dreadful sight to look at Segrave. " Richard, your own sister!"

He began to move towards me and I knew that I had come to the end of dreaming; the rest would be stark reality. Richard and his companion would lay hands on me and carry me into the black hole, where I would lie with Ruth.

As the room began to fade, I understood at last what the whispered words had meant.

"Not behind Farthing Wood." I said it in astonishment, as Richard took my hand. " Behind the panelling; that's what it meant. I should have known, for I listened to her dying."

As I fell, I was conscious of a violent pain in my head, but it was a momentary thing, and then the darkness which I had been waiting for came down like a cloud to cover me.

TEN

When I opened my eyes and found that I was lying down, I was convinced that I was in my coffin. It was seconds before I realised that I was not only alive, but comparatively unscathed. The softness beneath me was nothing so final as the satin lining of a long oak box, but merely Aunt Lucy's chintz-covered settee. It felt as though someone was pounding me on the head, and I winced as my exploring fingers encountered a sizeable lump just above one temple.

" My dear, are you all right?" It was Gillian Baxter, her worried face coming into focus, as she dabbed ineffectually at my brow with a damp cloth. " Alex, thank God you're safe. You poor child; how frightened you must have been."

I tried to sit up, partly to avoid Gillian's unwelcome ministrations, but it wasn't until a pair of strong arms came to my aid that I succeeded.

" Richard?"

He smiled, probably reading my thoughts.

" You struck your head when you fainted. Don't look like that. You're not in hell yet."

" I don't understand." I was bemused, gingerly moving my neck so that I could see who else was there. " What happened?"

David Baxter was by the window, Babs nearby. Even though I was confused, and nothing was making sense, it was obvious that Babs had changed. All her recent bombast had gone, and she was huddled in her chair as if she wanted to make herself invisible.

Then I noticed Max Mortimer sitting opposite me. He was very still, and all at once I realised how old he looked.

He had been so spruce, so upright, that I'd never connected
him with age, but now I could see how heavily the years sat
upon him.

"Richard, what happened? I thought you were going to
kill me."

"Yes." He was dry. "I rather gathered that, but I've no
sympathy for you. You deserved a fright for saying what you
did last night. Haven't you any sense at all?"

"I was told to say it."

It sounded inane and I wasn't surprised when he frowned.
"Told? By whom?"

This wasn't the time to try again to make Richard understand, and I ignored the question.

"Who was in the room with us? The other man, I mean?
I thought it was one of your friends." For a second, I was
back there, in near darkness, seeing eyes fixed on me with
purpose. I began to tremble. "That girl. . . ."

"Ruth." Richard was very controlled and I watched him
turn to Max. "That was my sister Ruth, and the other man
is no friend of mine. It was Mortimer, and he'll explain why
and how Ruth and Nan were killed. One of my servants has
gone for the police; meanwhile, Colonel, you can fill in the
gaps for me."

Max didn't move at first. He was the colour of clay, but
finally he passed a hand across his brow, as if he were wiping
away a dreadful sight.

"Yes, if you wish, for it doesn't matter any more. Tell
me, how did you know I was here?"

Richard squeezed my hand in comfort and sat down.

"Last night, an hour or so after I'd got home, I searched
Ruth's bedroom again. Both I and my servants had done so
on a number of occasions, because I felt sure there must be
something there which would give a hint of why she went,
and whether she went of her own accord. My sister always
kept a diary. Even small things were recorded in it, but I
couldn't find it. I haven't found it yet, but, whilst I was
looking last night, I knocked over a vase and broke it. In it,
there was a letter from your son, Colonel. It was clear that

Ruth had been with child and that the baby was his. He didn't want it, nor Ruth, but then, of course, you know that, don't you?

"Once I'd found that, I went straight to Chartley. You weren't there, but Gavin was. After a while, he was only too glad to tell me all that I wanted to know, including where you had gone, and the existence of the passageway behind Miss Leith's bedroom. He said you'd come to silence Alex. I don't understand that, because you knew Nan Ponsonby didn't kill herself, nor did she see anyone the day Ruth vanished. However, you will probably be able to explain it more coherently than your son was able to do."

"Gavin!" Max jerked, as if pulled by strings. "Where is he? If you've hurt him . . ."

"He's under lock and key with the others, and yes, I hurt him. But he'll recover from what I've done to him. Ruth won't, from what you did to her."

"Others?"

I couldn't bear the look on Richard's face, wanting to drive it away somehow.

"Yes, Alex. Your charming riding companion, Gavin, has no stomach for pain. He told me about the others, but let the colonel tell you the truth, and from the beginning. He owes you that much, at least."

Max said a few words under his breath and Richard bared his teeth.

"Be that as it may. I've satisfied your curiosity as to how I got here, now we'll hear what you've got to say. Miss Wycombe, will you get some coffee, please?"

Babs crept from the room without a word. I think she was as afraid of Segrave as Gavin had been.

"Well?"

Richard was implacable, and Mortimer sank back, his moment of anger done. In a way, he seemed almost relieved to talk about what had taken place, his voice tired and defeated, as if he'd travelled a long way down the road leading to purgatory.

In essence, the story was a simple one. Gavin had had an

affaire with the inexperienced Ruth, at a time when Segrave was away. Richard had got word of it and had warned Gavin that he would break every bone in his body if he went near Ruth once more. Shortly after, Segrave had left again for Europe, and Ruth had discovered that she was pregnant, begging Gavin to marry her.

Gavin knew Segrave wouldn't countenance such a thing, and he had gone completely to pieces at the thought of what Ruth's brother would do when he found out about the child.

"Gavin was petrified." Max seemed to be in a trance, living it all again. "His fear wasn't normal, and we couldn't calm him. I told him I'd speak to Segrave, but he wouldn't listen, for he was certain that Sir Richard had meant what he said. We tried to make him go abroad, out of it, but he said Segrave would find him wherever he went.

"We had to help him, or he'd have gone out of his mind, or taken his own life, and we couldn't let that happen. I don't expect you to understand what Athene and I feel for the boy. He's our only child; our son. We were prepared to do anything to save him, because he's all we've got."

I stole a look at Richard, but his face gave nothing away.

"We had no intention of killing Ruth." Max seemed to shudder, as if someone had walked over his grave. "That was never in our minds. There's an old woman in the village; a wise woman, they call her. She could have ended the pregnancy, and all would have been well, but Ruth wouldn't agree. She was too afraid."

I listened with disbelief as Mortimer went on.

When Ruth flatly refused to go to the wise woman, it had been decided to take her there by force. After it was all over, Max and Athene needed to ensure that, if Ruth ever told Richard the truth, her story would be shown to be a tissue of lies, so they concocted their own version of what had happened. Ruth had become pregnant by an unknown man and, of her own free will, had sought an abortion. She had told Athene, who had professed shock, but who had agreed to keep silent. The details were etched in carefully. A servant discovered what was going on, and soon others knew about

Ruth's predicament. Max and Athene wouldn't have been enough to bolster up the fabrication, if Ruth spoke to her brother, and so other respectable and reliable people had to be on hand to confirm the false story. Even Richard, confronted by facts given by a number of independent neighbours, would doubt his sister.

" And the others?"

Max held nothing back; completely truthful at the last.

Nadine Lancaster was the first. I felt a twinge of astonishment when I learned that the fastidious, proper Nadine had been Max's mistress. He had broken off their liaison two years before, but Nadine was still in love with him. Under her cool exterior, there had been deep passion, and the price for her help had been a resumption of the relationship.

Max had saved Geoffrey Thatcher's life when they had served in the army together. Mortimer had called in the debt and Geoffrey had paid it. Carlton wasn't a doctor at all. Max had always known that he was a charlatan, but he considered George was doing no real harm, with his sketchy knowledge of medicine. Athene had said that everyone in Winterhill was very healthy. Now it was different: Max's continued silence had to be paid for.

Gideon Woodbyrne, Max's ex-batman and loyal servant, worshipped his master, and then I remembered the look I'd seen pass between the two men on the night I first dined with the Mortimers. Gillian had said servants weren't like family: Woodbyrne and Mortimer had thought differently.

" Anyone else?" Richard was so icy that I almost shrank back, although his fury wasn't directed at me. " I think there was one other, wasn't there?"

" Yes." Max seemed to sag in his chair. " Yes, there was another; Dulcie Kipps."

" Dulcie!" It was the biggest shock of all. " You can't mean it! Dulcie wouldn't. . . ."

Max raised his head and looked at me, and I felt my blood run cold.

" How little you knew her! She was truly evil. I've met many people in my time. Criminals, perverts, men with twisted minds, the insane, but I've never encountered anyone like her before. What we did, or tried to do, was in order to help Gavin. What she did, she did for pleasure; she enjoyed it."

"What you tried to do?" Segrave was lighting a cigar and, despite what he was going through, his hands were as steady as a rock. "What you did do, surely?"

"I've told you; we had no intention of killing Ruth. Such a thing never occurred to us, but everything went wrong."

It seemed that on the night Ruth died, a message was sent to her to meet Gavin, who'd changed his mind about marrying her. Max and his friends were waiting for her to take her off to the wise woman. When Ruth saw the group coming towards her, she had fled, and it wasn't until she was well into Farthing Wood that they had caught her.

Max twitched, remembering bad things.

"We covered our faces, so she wouldn't see who we were. I was just about to tell Gideon to take her, when Kipps ran forward, and the next we knew was that Ruth had collapsed. We rushed over to her, but Dulcie had stabbed her in the stomach. Kipps had brought the knife with her and she'd always intended to use it. She found out, quite by chance, what we intended to do, and forced us to let her help. I told you; she was really wicked."

The group had been appalled, particularly when Dulcie had started to laugh, but they could see that Ruth was dying, and they had a completely new situation to face. They decided to bury her in the wood, but then they had heard the sound of horses, and people talking. It had taken them all by surprise; no one ever came near the wood, particularly at night, and they were frightened.

Dulcie, the stolid, scruffy menial of no account, had had her day. She had taken charge when the rest, scared out of their wits, had no idea what to do. All Max's experience on the field of battle hadn't helped him that night: it was a nightmare he couldn't cope with. Kipps had taken them back to Lucy's Cottage and shown them the passage which she'd discovered. They hadn't wanted to leave Ruth there, particularly as she was still alive, but there really wasn't any choice, unless they were prepared to give themselves up. None had been able to face that, and they had accepted Dulcie's solution, agreeing to return the next night and bury the body decently.

Their alarm and consternation increased when the very next morning Nan and Babs had arrived, and, later that same day, I too had come to Winterhill. They didn't doubt that Ruth was dead by then, but there was always the possibility that Nan or I might discover the passage behind my bedroom. It was necessary, therefore, for them to drive me away and they set out to create an aura of terror so that I should turn tail and run.

Babs came in with the coffee, and I was thankful for mine, trying to keep my hand steady as I remembered that when they had laid Ruth behind the wall she had still been breathing. I was watching Max, still unable to understand how he and the others had maintained a normal front, going about their daily business as if nothing had happened, concealing such dreadful deeds behind polite masks. Max and Athene had seemed to like me, and as for Gavin. . . .

They had started with the tale of Lucinda's madness, trying to convince me that she had said she would stay in her room after death. Evangeline Parr's insistence that the spirit lingering there was a man's had taken them all aback, but it hadn't deterred them.

The tales about the cottage had helped, and Dulcie had made sure I'd heard about them. It was she who had covered my frock with rabbit's blood, and had moved the portrait from the dining-room to my bedroom, gloating secretly, I had no doubt, when she had seen my shock. Both incidents were mentioned to me later, in connection with Lucinda's peculiarities. What had happened before was happening again: they piled fear upon fear, waiting for me to crack.

They hadn't tried to buy the cottage from Aunt Lucy, but Max and Athene thought it worth asking me to sell: an easy way to get rid of me, but I hadn't agreed.

When I proved hard to shift, they had grown really

worried and it seemed that all sense of caution and humanity had left them. None of them, except Kipps, had set out to kill, but, once started, the juggernaut couldn't be stopped. When Gavin was alone with his parents, he had been like a man possessed by devils, and I could sense Max's suffering as he described the Gavin the world saw, and the petrified wreck of a man he and Athene had to deal with behind closed doors. They had to try again.

They told Dulcie to put a powder in my hot milk. Carlton had had access to poisons, and provided what was needed, but that attempt failed too when the picture had fallen off the wall and Dulcie had smashed the glass.

Nan died because she had gone into my room and found Dulcie by the open panelling. Although Kipps was a monster, wholly indifferent to human life, she was both superstitious and credulous. She was beginning to worry about my stories of moaning sounds, and had started to wonder whether Ruth was really dead. She had gone to make sure, but Nan had disturbed her. She had had a knife in her apron pocket, and hadn't hesitated to use it, but Nan's death had to be explained.

As she had run from the cottage, Dulcie had met Athene. On hearing what had happened, Mrs Mortimer had kept her head, quick-witted as always. She had printed a note and told Dulcie to put it under the body; to see that Nan's fingers were round the handle of the knife, and that the panel was securely closed. Then she'd told Dulcie to go away, until it had been time for her to return from the errand on which she'd been sent.

They hadn't sought Nan's death, although her end helped to isolate me, but they'd made good use of it. Who did Nan Ponsonby care enough about to kill herself to protect? The finger had pointed directly at me.

"But if Athene wrote the note under Nan's body, you knew she hadn't seen anyone." I was in misery, remembering Nan and how she had looked that last day. "Why did you come here tonight? You must have been aware that I wasn't telling the truth."

Mortimer shrugged.

" Yes, we were sure, at least we were when you first spoke. Later, Gavin began to fret and torment himself in case it had been your maid in the wood that night, and somehow you'd just found out."

" The sound of horses, and people? Nan?"

" It sounds ridiculous, I know, but you don't know what Gavin has been like. In any event, it was time we moved Ruth's body and, since you wouldn't go voluntarily, we had to find another way."

I was cold right through, listening to Mortimer pronounce my death sentence.

" What would you have done? And what about Babs and Sheena?"

" When you were dead, I would have put you with Ruth until Miss Wycombe had gone home, as obviously she would have had to do. Sheena would have been no problem."

" I can't believe what you're saying." I felt ill, hardly able still to take in that the bluff, jovial Max had been pre-pared to make away with me. " Had you no remorse? No feeling at all?"

" Yes." Mortimer found the strength at last to face Richard. " You must believe that at first we didn't intend to kill your sister, but when that lunatic girl stabbed her every-thing got out of hand, and, once started, there was no end to it. We did panic, I admit. It all happened so quickly, and Kipps seemed to drive us along, and then it was too late. We hadn't expected to injure you, Miss Leith. We thought you'd be so afraid that you'd go."

He sighed and looked round the room.

" Ruth never came here, you know. For some reason, she hated this cottage. We invented the tale of her friendship with Miss Oakley, and the second will, to throw suspicion on Miss Leith. I'm sure, Sir Richard, that you wondered about her, didn't you?"

" For a short while, but quite soon I realised that she had had nothing to do with Ruth's disappearance. It wasn't a matter of logic or reason, but pure instinct. I just knew."

For a second, Max was ironically amused.

" A sound instinct, and when we told Miss Leith that you'd inherit your grandmother's money if Ruth died before she married and had a child, she suspected you, didn't you, Miss Leith?" He glanced at Gillian. " We primed Mrs Baxter with that piece of gossip, and she was quick to pass it on."

Gillian was crying, but I was filled with shame because of what I'd thought of Richard.

" Yes, I did suspect Richard. It wasn't true about the fortune then?"

" No." Richard must have known how I was feeling, for he leaned over and held my hand. " It was left to me, not Ruth."

" But I did think you were guilty." I had to purge my soul. " When you stepped out of that passage tonight, I thought you were going to kill me. I thought you and your friends had killed Ruth. Oh, Richard, I'm so very sorry."

He touched my fingers with his lips.

" Don't be: I understand. In such circumstances, it's no wonder that you doubted me."

I wanted to hold him close to me, but I couldn't in front of Max. It would have soiled what I felt, and there were other things I wanted to know.

" Colonel, was Aunt Lucy really mad? Did she tell Dr Carlton she wouldn't leave the cottage when she died?"

" No, she was normal enough, and she said nothing like that to George. It was simply part of our efforts to make you go. We wanted you to believe you were going out of your mind, like Miss Oakley."

I felt Richard's hand tighten on mine, so hard that I nearly cried out.

" You almost succeeded," I said shakily. " There were times when . . ."

I broke off. Mortimer wouldn't have the satisfaction of seeing my weakness.

" At one time, I thought it might be Babs."

I gave Babs an apologetic smile, but I don't think she saw

it. She was weeping, completely shattered in the face of true evil. Her sins had been petty ones. She had been jealous of me, and had longed to own the cottage. When I began to show signs of fear, she had taken advantage of it, almost intoxicated with power when I started to break down.

"I thought she might have been responsible for the noises." I turned back to Max. "Who attacked me in the wood?"

My lips were stiff, because I was back there, in the half-light, alone amongst the trees.

"Gideon." Mortimer was sombre. "He would have finished you off then, but he was disturbed. He said he heard voices again, and he ran." He was frowning. "We never found out who was there that day, nor the night Ruth died. No one goes to Farthing Wood, and all the villagers swear there were no strangers passing through on either occasion. It's a mystery."

"Then which of you led me home? If Woodbyrne set out to kill me, why did one of you help me back to the cottage?"

Max's frown deepened.

"Help you back? I don't know what you mean."

"You must do! Someone was in the wood when I woke up. They told me to follow them. I was completely lost, and it was getting very dark. If they hadn't been there, I don't know what I would have done."

"None of us helped you." Max was eyeing me dubiously. "Perhaps you just thought you heard someone."

"I can assure you I didn't." I was indignant. "And, after all, you heard voices in the wood yourselves. So did I."

He didn't bother to argue.

"And the smell, the moans, the whispering and the heart-beat? How did Dulcie manage those? I assume it was Dulcie, since she was the only one of you inside the cottage."

Mortimer was pulling his lower lip thoughtfully and it was clear that he was telling the truth when he answered.

"I'm afraid I've no idea what you're talking about. Dulcie wouldn't have done anything except on my orders. After that first night, I told her I would have no more of her madness. I said I expected total obedience, or she'd pay the consequences. She was sufficiently scared of me to listen. No, it wasn't Kipps."

" But you knew about the sounds." I could feel myself growing tense. I had expected Mortimer to confirm that Dulcie was to blame, but it was obvious that she hadn't been. I didn't want to think about an alternative. " Dulcie knew about them; she must have told you. Babs, that's true, isn't it? You and Nan and Dulcie all knew about the smell and the sounds."

" Well . . . yes." Babs blew her nose, looking at me anxiously, trying to appease me. " We knew what you said, but we didn't hear anything ourselves."

" Colonel! You knew, didn't you?"

" Kipps mentioned you'd complained about noises, yes, but I didn't take much notice. Since we'd set out to frighten you away, I assumed you'd grown nervous and were imagining things. It was all in your mind."

" No, it wasn't!" It was like a new nightmare and I held on to Richard's hand to keep myself calm. " I know I wasn't imagining those things. The moaning must have been Ruth. Richard! She was in agony for so long, and I didn't realise it."

He got up, holding me against him, ignoring the others.

" Don't, my darling, don't. Ruth would have been dead within an hour, probably before that. I've seen the wound. Whatever you think you heard, it wasn't her."

Gillian's tears were still trickling down her cheeks.

" Poor child; oh, poor little Ruth."

" But what else could it have been?" I didn't want to accept Max's word; I wanted a logical answer. " Colonel, you've admitted everything else, so why don't you tell me the rest? One of you must have. . . ."

" We didn't." He closed the subject bluntly. " Woman's nerves; that's all."

" Where is Kipps now?" Richard released me. " She's not with your wife and son, so I take it she got away. Well, the police will find her in due course."

" Yes, they will." Mortimer sounded even more exhausted as if the life were draining out of him. " I'll tell them where to look. She's buried under the laurel-bushes on the north side of my garden."

" What! "

" Yes, in the end, even she lost her nerve and her taste for blood. She packed her bag and came to me. She kept talking about a picture which had fallen off the wall, gibbering like an idiot, and saying she must go to the wise woman for help. She would have betrayed us and I couldn't let that happen; not after all we'd gone through. I did try to pacify her, I swear. I offered her money to go away, perhaps to London, but she wouldn't listen. In the end, I lost my temper and strangled her."

" Good God! "

Max gave a short laugh.

" You're shocked, Sir Richard? You'd be surprised how easy taking life is once one has started, although, as I've said, nothing was further from our thoughts when we began. We aren't naturally violent people. We didn't want to harm your sister, and if she'd agreed to our proposal she'd be alive today. We all liked her, but Gavin had to be saved. He was the one who mattered."

" Not to me."

Segrave was very quiet.

" No, of course not to you. We were sorry about Miss Ponsonby too, but I suppose Dulcie had no choice. She was caught red-handed."

" Why did Gavin pay so much attention to me?" I intervened, because I could feel Richard's anger growing. It was almost as though his emotion were my emotion; as if we were one person. " He seemed so fond of me, but I suppose that was untrue as well."

" It was at first. We told him to make a fuss of you; to become a close friend. That way, he could keep an eye on you and tell us how you were reacting."

I was glad. Gavin hadn't cared tuppence about me; it eased my conscience, but Max hadn't finished.

" He also tried to convince you that Miss Wycombe hated you and meant you harm. She was an ideal suspect and I gather from what you say that you believed my son's warning."

" Yes, I did. He played his part well."

Max ignored my bitterness.

" If he'd been able to get you to send your companion away, you'd have been more vulnerable, particularly after Miss Ponsonby died. Almost alone, in fact, but things didn't quite work out as Athene and I had planned."

" Oh?"

Mortimer looked at me, letting his glance move slowly over me.

" No, that is the greatest irony of all. He fell in love with you, you see. Athene and I and the others did terrible things to save him from the consequences of an *affaire* with Segrave's sister, and all the while he was becoming besotted by you. It was as if he were leading a double life. Happy when he was with you; despairing and half-mad when he was with us."

" I wasn't in love with him, Colonel Mortimer."

" I know that." Max almost smiled. " Athene made it clear to me where your affections lay."

I blushed and couldn't look at Richard.

We had finished our coffee, and Gillian was putting the cups on the tray, looking ten years older. She couldn't sit still and kept dropping spoons and clattering saucers until her husband got up to help her.

When the police finally came, Mortimer straightened his shoulders, standing like the soldier he had once been. He was going to his death, ultimately, but he had courage, unlike his son.

" It is useless for me to say I'm sorry." He met Richard's eyes without flinching. " It all seemed so simple at the start. None of us had any notion it would turn out as it did."

Segrave didn't answer, but I had to make one more attempt to solve my own riddle.

" Colonel, please!"

" Yes?"

" You've nothing to lose now; nothing at all. Won't you tell me the real truth about those noises, and who led me out of the wood? It had to be one of you; there wasn't anyone else it could have been."

He considered me for some time, until the sergeant at the door began to cough pointedly.

" As you say, I've nothing to lose, except my life, and somehow that doesn't seem important any more. Gavin was my life, but I failed him."

" Not as much as he failed you."

" No, perhaps not. All our love and devotion couldn't make a man of him, but one loves one's child, with all its faults. Athene and I didn't judge him. No, Miss Leith, if I knew the answer to your questions I would tell you, but I don't. Whatever you believe you heard, you can rest assured it was nothing to do with us."

Richard left with Max and the police, whilst the Baxters went to the kitchen to try to explain to Sheena what had happened. Gillian, kind as always, was going to offer her a position in her own household.

" Babs, there are some questions I want to ask you too."

She had stopped crying and was waiting for my anger to spill over her. There was no need for her to tell me what she'd tried to do, for I knew, and she was aware of it. She sat patiently, ready to accept what was coming.

She confessed quite freely that she had lied about the letter Lucy was supposed to have sent me, and about the portrait of my aunt which she'd said was so like me.

" I was jealous," she finished in a small voice, " and I'm so ashamed because you and your mother have always been so good to me, and this is how I've repaid you. I can't explain why I did it, really. It was just that I adored this cottage, and you began to be different. You weren't sure of yourself, as you normally are, and then you started to be afraid. I found that I could make you do what I wanted, and for the first time in my life I felt important."

I nodded.

" Yes, I think I understand. And the green surah dress:
you did wear that, didn't you? I thought I was going out of
my mind when I came home that day and you were wearing
a frock of your own, pretending you'd never seen the gown
I was talking about."

She reddened.

" Yes, I did wear it, and I lied to you. Just after you'd
gone out that day, a letter came from my father telling me
I had to go home at once to help my mother, because three
of the children were ill. I do hate it so at home, Alex. We're
poor; so very poor. Mother can't manage things, and Father
is so stern. I had to convince you that you needed me, so
I could write to my father and tell him I couldn't leave you,
but I knew then that I had to stop being hateful to you and
taking your things, so I put the dress away."

I touched her hand as she went off to pack. I don't think
I would ever grow fond of Babs, but I think I realised at
that moment the temptation which had been dangled in
front of her. Perhaps in her place, I would have done the
same.

Richard came back, looking sad, rather than angry, and
I had to choose my words carefully.

" I don't know what to say; it is such a terrible thing. But
I do believe Colonel Mortimer when he said they didn't
intend to hurt her."

His eyes were sightless; he was a long way away.

" Not hurt her?" He came back from his private hell.
" They were going to drag a seventeen-year-old girl to a dirty
old woman, Megs Ambler. I know her; she lives in a hovel
no better than a cesspool. If Ruth had survived what Megs
was going to do to her, the rest of them would have made
sure I wouldn't have believed her story, if ever she had
spoken to me about it. My poor Ruth; she was too young to
realise what she was getting into with young Mortimer, but
Max was right. I wouldn't have taken her word against
theirs, and I'll never forgive myself."

" But Ruth didn't know that. Dearest, she doesn't . . .
didn't know that."

" But I do."

We sat quietly for a while, for he wasn't ready yet to be comforted. I didn't want to add to his burdens, but I had to get it over with.

" I didn't imagine those things." I forced myself to be very calm. " I did hear noises and there really was a smell."

He said nothing.

" I don't know whether it was Aunt Lucy, or Evangeline Parr's man, but, whoever it was, they were trying to tell me about Ruth, but I didn't understand."

" There are always foolish women like Miss Parr." He opened his eyes and looked at me. " What you are trying to make me believe is beyond all reason. If there were noises and a smell, which I don't accept, they would have been connected with the man Miss Parr spoke of : they wouldn't have been anything to do with Ruth. When the woman visited the cottage, and said she sensed someone, Ruth was alive and well, at The Hall."

" The man was forewarning her."

" Oh really!"

" And after Ruth was dead he, if it was the man, tried to tell me what happened and where to find her."

I almost added that the warning Evangeline had had was rather like my dreams, but I thought dreams were more than Richard could have tolerated just at that moment.

" It is utterly impossible. Alex, I've listened to enough of this. You were conditioned to hear things. Local tales, and Max and the rest of them making sure you believed in them."

I made one last effort.

" Perhaps, but why should the manifestation be as it was? You must admit it fits Ruth's death."

I couldn't tell Richard all that I had experienced. The shadow on the wall; the sense of being loved. Some things I would always have to keep to myself, and it was clear that Richard wasn't prepared to let me go on, and so I went back to Max.

" I still can't believe it," I said unhappily. " Max, Athene,

Nadine. They seemed so ordinary; so normal. As for
Kipps." I shuddered. " I can't bear to think about her. She
enjoyed killing . . . and . . . Nan . . ."

He rose at once, pulling me to my feet.

" Don't think about Kipps or the others; it's over now.
You can't bring Ruth back, my dearest, lovely Alex. All our
tears and regrets won't make her live again. Tell me, when
did you know that you loved me?"

I answered promptly, and with total honesty, for this was
no time to be coy.

" From the first moment I saw you. You looked so cold
and angry, and I was afraid of you, but it didn't make any
difference. I knew at once what had happened; there was no
mistaking it, although I thought you disliked me. You must
think me a complete wanton."

He took my face between his hands, saying nothing for
a long while.

" No, I think you're beautiful, and brave to tell me the
truth."

" Does it help?"

" Oh yes. Love heals quicker than anything else. And I
didn't dislike you; it was the same for me. Once I'd seen
you, there could be nobody else for me. Marry me, Alex,
and help me to lay my ghost."

His second kiss was as wonderful as the first and I went
upstairs wholly and marvellously contented, in spite of sorrow, shock, fear and exposure to dreadful violence. It was
also a relief to learn that Richard's father was entirely sane,
and merely lived in Switzerland because of a chest condition.

On the landing, I paused, a quiver striking through my
happiness. Max and his friends had heard the sound of
horses, and people talking in the wood; Woodbyrne had
heard voices too, and so had I. Yet there had been no
strangers about, and the locals never went into Farthing
Wood. I doubted if there had been any real people in the
wood the night Ruth died, or later. I felt a quick grue. It had
to be something else.

In my room, I stood for a moment before the portrait,

curiously dismayed, feeling a sudden and very deep sense of loss. There wasn't really any difference which I could have explained to anyone, yet the portrait wasn't the same.

The eyes were simply daubs of blue paint, the mouth a streak of crimson. It wasn't alive any more; it was just a picture. I turned away, and started to pack a small valise. It had always been just a picture and, if Richard had to forget his ghost, I had to forget Lucinda's bedroom, and what it might contain.

At the gate, an old man was waiting for us.

"This is Simeon New," said Richard. "You remember that I told you he thought he'd seen Ruth run into the cottage."

"Very sorry, Miss, that I am." New was apologetic, ducking his head. "I could 'ave sworn it were Miss Ruth, but it must 'ave been Dulcie Kipps after all. Nasty girl, that one. I 'ated 'er, even when she were a child. Always hurtin' things, she was."

"You've lived here all your life, I understand?" I wouldn't let Dulcie creep back into my mind. "You knew my great-aunt, of course."

"I did that. Nice old body. I've 'eard talk recently that she weren't right in the 'ead, but it's not true. Bright as a button, right up to the end."

"She died slowly though, and in pain." I was crying inside for Lucy. "Dulcie said she suffered terribly towards the end."

"Lyin' little tyke!" New was fierce. "That's what she told others too, but it weren't so. I've ways of makin' meself understood to Sheena, and she to me. Yer aunt went quite sudden and ever so peaceful."

"So she didn't moan, or . . ."

"That's enough, Alex." Richard was curt. "Get into the carriage."

I obeyed meekly, as he went back to check that the back door was secure.

"Well, Simeon." I leaned down and put a few coins in his hand. "Thank you for telling me that. I'm glad she died quietly, and, after all, she was lucky in one way. She did have a cottage named after her, didn't she?"

" Eh?"

Simeon was counting the money, looking vague.

" The cottage." I was patient, for he was very old. " It was named after her."

He let out a cackle.

" Bless yer, Miss, it weren't named for 'er. Been called Lucy's Cottage for more'un five 'undred years; mebbee longer. Lucifer's Cottage, that's whose it is. Always was; always will be. They calls 'im Lucy for short around these parts. People don't come 'ere 'cos they know it's 'is, see. 'E let yer aunt bide in it for a while, but 'e never left it 'imself. I reckon Miss Oakley knew that."

He gave me a toothless grin and ambled off, while I sank back completely stunned.

I dared not say anything to Richard as he joined me and took the reins. He wouldn't have believed me and I couldn't bear him to be angry with me again.

As we moved off, I clenched my hands. Very faint, as before, but I could hear it, nevertheless.

" Good-bye, my lovely, good-bye. Come back one day."

I said wonderingly:

" He saved my life twice. Why? Oh, how I wish I knew why!"

" Mm?"

Richard was inattentive, his mind on the horses, and a sharp bend ahead.

" It's nothing. I was only saying farewell to my cottage, for I don't suppose I shall ever see it again."

But as we turned and trotted out on to the road to Shottley I wasn't so sure. Perhaps, one day, many years hence, I would come back to Winterhill after all, and Lucy's Cottage would still be there, just as it had been for centuries. Older, shabbier, shunned and turned in upon itself, yet not completely deserted.

He would be there, waiting; waiting for me.